The Hope and Melvin of Humanity
and Other Surprising Short Stories

Also, by Jonathan J Foster

Where Was God on the Worst Day of My Life

Death, Hope, and the Laughter of God: An Unlikely Title About the Unlikely Path Where God Finds Us

Questions about Sexuality that Got Me Uninvited from My Denomination

The Hope and Melvin of Humanity and Other Surprising Short Stories

Jonathan J Foster

www.jonathanfosteronline.com

© 2021 Jonathan J Foster

ISBN : 978-1-7376649-0-1 (print)

ISBN : 978-1-7376649-1-8 (ePub)

Ebook/Print formatting: booknook.biz

Cover: Quinn Carr, carrdiacdesign

Editing: Julie Miller, editorialdepartment.com

The universe humans like the rosebud flowers.

—*Alan Watts*

Table of Contents

Golden Point

Theogad was a young king with a coastal monarchy extending from The Point of Hope in the North, to The Hopeful Point in the South, across many points all along the way. At no point, though, was there anything as important as the city of Golden Point, a place where golden sunsets lit up the cliffs, spires, and high-rises at the end of each royal day.

In its youth Golden Point was content and unassuming, loosely scattered among beaches and foothills, but with its ascension up and into mountains and cliffs, it developed a certain ambition. Driving up the winding and circular roads, like rings in a tree, one could mark the maturation. Below, it was simple buildings, wooden and stoned. Above, it was superstructures, glassed and alloyed, pointing and angling to get ahead in commerce, trade, politics, and religion.

The people of Golden Point were religiously devoted to their God and land. It was this devotion that inspired them annually to hold a week-long festival culminating at the highest cliffs of Golden Point called *The Point of Sacrifice and New Beginnings for Everyone.*

It was there in the cliffs, where the people joined the king in what was always a picture-perfect moment. They would feel the embrace of the day's last sunlight, sense the loving and pinkish clouds above, hear the strong but affectionate breakers below, marvel at the golden hue illuminating the cliffs all around, and finally witness the king, as he stepped out onto the highest point of the cliff and flung three puppies and a kitten down onto the rocks below. After a moment of silence, thanking God for receiving their offering, the people would break out into celebration.

It was a joyful time of song and dance throughout Golden Point and the entire kingdom.

. . . . .

"But why puppies?" cried LaQueesha.

"Yeah," chimed Milton, "Why does it have to be puppies and kittens? They're *sooo* cute."

Ms. Burkenlips rolled her eyes. She had heard it all before. *What are they teaching these kids at home? Do I have to do everything? For crying out loud, they're in second grade!*

Other kids were clamoring for answers now, "Why the puppies? Why kittens? They are so cute!"

Lucius yelled, "We should throw lizards or snakes off the cliff! That'd be way better!"

"Yes," other children chimed in, "Lizards and snakes!" They began jumping and chanting until the entire class was singing and laughing, in unison, "Lizards and snakes! Lizards and snakes!"

"Hush, hush! Everyone, please sit down." Ms. Burkenlips alternated pressing her palms against her skirt, then forehead, subconsciously attempting to straighten wrinkles. "I know the puppies are cute and *that's* the point. God doesn't want ugly puppies. Honestly, what are you kids thinking? The puppies have to be cute for it to make a real difference. You can't offer up ugly animals!"

. . . . .

King Theogad rubbed his own shoulder while conversing with the nation's highest religious office. "Bishop Claxon, I understand the festival is a long-standing tradition, but has anyone ever thought about thinking through this differently?"

"Thinking differently?" replied Bishop Claxon. And then again, "Thinking *differently*?"

Theogad sighed. He knew the bishop was frustrated

when he repeated a question. It gave him time to think of a response. The more frustrated the bishop grew, the more often he would repeat a question. Theogad had once heard the bishop repeat a question thirteen times before answering.

"Dear King Theogad"—the bishop drew close to Theogad and flicked imaginary dust off the king's shoulders—"when my grandfather was a boy, he used to collect honey for a living. He had a routine. Each day."

Theogad rolled his eyes internally.

The bishop turned abruptly while pulling down and straightening his tunic, "Up at dawn. Breakfast. Bee suit and mask on. Make the rounds. Draw the honey." The bishop enumerated each point with a crisp tap of his thumb and fingers together as he marched in a circle. "He always felt it wasn't a good morning's work unless he was stung, five times at least. I would meet him for lunch in the summers and he would show me the welts." The bishop stopped marching and stared up into the furthest corner of the vaulted ceiling, his eyes growing moist. Theogad guessed the bishop was reminiscing about the beautiful, throbbing outgrowths of pain on his father's arm.

Theogad leaned in front of him, catching his attention, "What does this have to do with thinking differently?"

The bishop, startled, said, "Ah yes, well, I would ask my

father if he ever considered wearing a different suit. One to prevent so much stinging."

"And?" Theogad drew the word out slowly.

"Ha, 'Of course not,' he would reply." He punctuated the air with a turn of his fist. "'It's a part of the beekeeping business. It's the pain that reminds you of the work. It's the fear that keeps you alive, on your toes. A new bee suit would take away the fear. Fear is what drives the business, son.'" The bishop's gaze wandered off again, as if he were surrounded by vast fields of bees and honey.

Theogad started to follow the bishop's gaze, then shook his head. "Wait," he said slowly, "this is why we shouldn't approach *The Point of Sacrifice and New Beginnings for Everyone* any differently than we have in the past? This is why we should continue to fling puppies and kittens off cliffs? Because if we didn't, there would be no more fear?"

"Yes," the bishop hopped up on one foot as he replied. "Yes, you are finally getting it! This is what my wise father was trying to teach me. It's the new ideas that get you into trouble. It's obvious God is more powerful than us, more intelligent than us, and able to do anything he wants to us. Theogad, He is the Almighty." The bishop stretched his arms out wide to accentuate God's almighty-ness. "Our sacrifices must be *serious*. We must make them *count*. Surely you know this. It's in our act of *flinging* those puppies that God sees our commitment, true and straight."

Then Bishop Claxon crouched slightly and placed one hand on Theogad. He closed his eyes and extended his other. "King Theogad, I want you to picture yourself out on that cliff ... can you see it, Theogad? Can you see yourself flinging those animals?

Theogad stared blankly at the cleric's closed eyes.

"Yes, yes, you can see it there. Now ... see the fear in the eyes of those animals flying through the air off into the darkness ... can you picture it, Theogad?" Squeezing Theogad's arm, he asked again, "*Can you?*"

Theogad raised his eyebrows at the sharpness of the man's grip. He looked down at the rangy and bejeweled fingers clasping his arm, then back at the bishop, and slowly nodded.

The bishop opened one eye to see Theogad nodding. "Yes, you can. Good."

Squeezing his eye shut quickly, he said, "Now turn—in slow motion—and see that same fear reflected, in the eyes of the all the children watching." His voice rose. "There at the cliffs, all throughout Golden Point, all throughout our glorious Kingdom."

Claxon opened his eyes, suddenly and wild. "This is a *good* thing, Theogad. It keeps us on our toes." Shaking a fist in the air, he added, "It's the *pain* and *fear* that let us know we're doing the right work."

The bishop raised his chin, spun on his heels, and as he exited, said, "Yes! Good work, Theogad!"

Theogad watched the bishop's back disappear down the hallway.

. . . . .

The people throughout the kingdom reserved a special place in their hearts for puppies and kittens. Those adorable little creatures were treated with more affection than all other animals. No one paid any attention to hamsters or hermit crabs, goldfish or gerbils. No, it was the puppies and kittens that garnered all the attention.

And if this was true throughout the kingdom, it was even more true the closer one got to Golden Point. The animal business thrived in the nation's most important city. More veterinarians lived per square mile in Golden Point than anywhere else in the country. Animal groomers, walkers, excrement picker-uppers, and dieticians as well.

And if the reverence of dogs and cats increased in ever-tightening concentric circles from the outskirts of the kingdom to Golden Point, well, then it absolutely turned obsessive as one made their way further up and into the center of the city. And there in the middle of the city, the focal point of the nation, the nucleus of all that animated Golden Point's tradition, sat the jewel of the nation: Kennel Point.

Ah yes, Kennel Point, that holiest of kennels directed by the church, protected by the military, and adored by the nation.

Kennel Point was the nation's premiere kennel. Golden Point's citizens brought their most prized dogs and cats to the kennel, paying large sums of money in the hopes it would be *their* pet to sire or birth the baby animals thrown off the cliff. It was quite an honor to be associated in any way with a sacrificial puppy or kitten.

One solitary puppy was offered in the old days, but, over time, God revealed He was unsatisfied with just one. It had to be two, *yea,* even three.

Then, thankfully, in a series of divinely inspired revelations, it was determined breed was important as well. Whereas in ancient and uncultured times, the king threw all kinds of dogs off the cliff, by King Theogad's reign, it was widely understood that only Pomeranian, basset hound, and golden retriever puppies would serve the purpose.

A kitten was thrown in for good measure in later years, but honestly, there didn't seem to be as much concern about the cat breed. It appeared God wasn't that impressed with cats anyhow. It was the puppies that really did the trick.

. . . . .

"Any questions?" Hands shot up all over the auditorium

where Dr. Cymbalgong taught from within the nation's most prestigious seminary. "Yes"—he peered into the top corners of the room—"OK, there in the back. Is that Jose?"

Jose, a studious and responsible seminarian, with fingers hovering just above his laptop, carefully asked, "Are there a certain number of rocks the puppies must hit before landing in the bay? How can we be certain they have suffered enough?"

"Excellent question, Jose." Dr. Cymbalgong was in his element. He was a specialist in the field of all things animal and expiation.

"Yes, yes," he mused while massaging his chin with thumb and index finger. "You are referring to, of course, what we call the 'Division of Labor.'" He walked across the front of the room with hands clasped behind his back as the room filled with the clickity-clack of keyboards rushing to type: *D-i-v-i-s-i-o-n -o-f -La-b-o-r.*

"Division of Labor, that is, how to divide and quantify the pain to ensure enough suffering takes place for God to be satisfied. Yes, there has been considerable debate about this over the years, but as was argued in the *Summit of Salvation*, then upheld in the *Council of Castigation*," he held his finger up in the air and waited for a wave of clickety-clacks to grow louder and then crest. And as if grabbing a surfboard, the very moment the volume began its downward movement, he dropped his hands and continued, "There must be a minimum of four rocks and/or otherwise sharp objects the animals collide with on their way to the sea." He crouched through the curl of attention all around him. "There must be *suffering*." Then louder as if shouting over the noise of surf washing up onto the shore, he said, "and it must be *painful*."

He stood for a moment, reacclimating to solid ground, then jogged over to the other side of the room to grab his laptop. He snatched it, flipping his hand, flinging a projection up onto the screen. It was a flawlessly executed flip and fling. "God is *very* holy and deserves suffering."

Then he whipped out a stylus and begin drawing, "Four rocks will ensure breakage of bones and rupturing of organs before the animal drowns in the water," accompanying his teaching in real time by a flurry of diagrams, charts, and designs. "If there are more rocks, well, that is even better, but four will suffice."

Finished, he tossed the tablet onto his desk and chucked the stylus over his shoulders as he walked to the middle of the room, wiping forelocks falling across his forehead (with his forearm, no less). He squared himself, gesturing to the screen behind him with arms wide open, and with a flourish said, "This is good and pleasing to God." He dropped his head.

A couple of the students clapped. Others furiously typed. Some held phones and tablets up to take pictures of the diagrams from a variety of different angles. Others tapped chins with pencils as they paced back and forth and studied the screen. One of the students called their parents right there in the classroom to personally thank them for funding such a university experience. Yes, students, moms, and dads all around the kingdom were pleased with all that was being taught at the seminary.

. . . . .

King Theogad waited in the back of a dark, unmarked SUV in the upper cliffs and echelons of Golden Point the day before the festival. A group of security guards fanned outward while one opened Theogad's door. He unfolded his legs and stepped out onto the grounds of *The Point of Sacrifice and New Beginnings for Everyone*.

He walked to the edge of the cliff to peer over, taking in a breath of clean coastal air. Then soaking up the afternoon sun, he took in the view from left to right, turning slowly until his gaze was interrupted by a group that included Bishop Claxon, Kennel Point's CEO, and a small number of high-ranking soldiers. Theogad caught sight of the huddle as it broke position and made its way through a small army of people preparing the site for the forthcoming festivities. A wordless colonel slipped from the group with a subdivision of soldiers and gained Theogad's attention.

He escorted Theogad through the gates and onto the cliff. The king looked around, out over the waters, then leaned back to ask the colonel quietly, "Do you know what we are doing here today?"

"Sir"—the colonel's thick eyebrows were unmoving, like sleeping caterpillars—"I'm here to dispense detailed instructions regarding the sacred puppy fling that will take place at tomorrow's ceremony."

"Yes, my King," Bishop Claxon chimed in as he approached. "We must ensure you have the proper form."

Theogad stood quietly for a moment snapping his fingers with a rhythmic clapping sound of fist into palm of the other hand.

Bishop Claxon draped an arm around the young king's shoulders, shielding Theogad's countenance from observers. "This is your moment, Theogad. You can't just gently drop these animals over the edge. You have to really give them a whirl." Clapping Theogad on the back, he turned and said, "Colonel, please proceed."

"Yes, sir." The colonel flicked his hand. Immediately, two soldiers appeared with an unmarked trunk. They sat the trunk down at Theogad's feet, saluted, and backed away.

Another solider approached the colonel. They extended a tablet with a locked screen in need of an eighteen-digit password. The colonel, tongue sticking out in concentration, typed in Throwthatpuppy1234!, making sure to capitalize the first T. When he hit enter, the trunk opened with a pneumatic-sounding *whoosh* and revealed a golden cage within.

The cage lifted, revealing a variety of stuffed-animal puppies and kittens serving as stand-ins for the real thing. The colonel stepped forward, extracted one of the surrogate victims, then in rapid succession demonstrated the proper way of holding, the specific angle of flinging, the exact moment of disengaging, the desired trajectory of arcing, so that maximum victimization would be enacted. He launched stuffed animal after stuffed animal with laserlike precision.

The colonel finished his demonstration, then repositioned himself next to Theogad reverently, solemnly, quietly, as if the moment needed space. Theogad looked at him standing at attention, chest rising and falling, perspiration developing upon the bridge of his nose. He looked at the colonel, then out over the cliff, then back to the colonel. "Did you go to school for this?"

"Sir?" The colonel asked, countenance unaffected except for the slightest dart of his eyes.

"How long did it take you to learn all this?"

"Sir, I've spent my entire adult life in training for the sacrificial animal fling."

Theogad looked up into the sky and squinted while attempting to calculate the number of dollars the kingdom had spent on training men like this colonel to fling puppies.

"Sir"—the colonel held out several stuffed animals—"we should probably practice for tomorrow."

Theogad looked at him, then down at the animals. He leaned over to make sure he gained access to the colonel's eyes by looking up and under his ample eyebrows and said, "No thank you, Colonel. I think I understand."

The colonel turned his head slightly, then immediately straightened. He stood mutely, hands extended, still full of stuffed animals. Theogad turned and headed back to his car. Bishop Claxon glanced at his colleagues, began to say something, but then rushed to follow the king.

. . . . .

The following morning the sun cast its light through the king's bedroom windows and drapes, across marble floors and up onto the king's bed, where it found the king awake and staring at the vaulted ceiling. He blinked in the morning's rays, then swung his feet off the bed. He put his head in his hands for a moment, then began preparations for the day: most exciting for his nation, most dreadful for him.

Theogad's morning and afternoon were packed with activity. Breakfast with the military leaders. A tour of Kennel

Point, including the ceremonial viewing of runner-up cutest puppies and kittens with a dozen local elementary-age children. Lunch with a handful of politicians and leading dog trainers. And then the midafternoon service, televised kingdom-wide, in the nation's oldest cathedral.

Following the service, security escorted the king out the building and past a line of SUVs to a flag-bearing limousine with the back door open. An unmarked, rubbernecking man in dark sunglasses deposited Theogad into the car, closed the door, and thumped the roof three times. The entourage began the drive up and into the mountains, cliffs, and *The Point of Sacrifice and New Beginnings for Everyone.*

Theogad's car was full of people and noise. The bishop sat on the bench opposite Theogad fidgeting with his seatbelt, tapping his foot, and barking out last-minute instructions to aides and security.

Theogad leaned his head up against the window and willed the bishop's nervous energy to fade out of his mind. He watched the crowds lining the road, families throwing Frisbees, and the elderly holding babies. He recalled faces of the school-aged children he had been with that morning. He watched the sky and felt his face peppered with sunlight, intermittent between trees and buildings, clouds and promontories. He noted the sun's path west, as it set.

He cracked the back window, allowing the breeze to gain access, smelling the sea and the food being grilled, baked, and served. He listened to the live music, fading in and out around every twist and turn. And for the first time in days, he smiled. He smiled, breathed, and prayed.

The vehicle slowed and then stopped. Theogad's smiling stopped as well. He heard—or more accurately, felt—the throbbing of the crowd's anticipation. He exhaled a long, steady stream of air. When his door opened, he stepped out and onto the entryway of *The Point of Sacrifice and New Beginnings for Everyone*. He paused to see thousands of people crowded behind barricades up and down the street, up above on the cliffs, spilling out of windows, and in restaurants across the intersection, in balloons flying overhead, plus paratroopers jumping from airplanes and large screens projecting the faces of people from all around the kingdom.

A golden hue enveloped him, the people, and the surroundings as he walked to the edge of *The Point of Sacrifice and New Beginnings for Everyone*. He saw the colonel and his soldiers awaiting his arrival. The colonel inputted the unlock code as he approached. He heard the pneumatic *whoosh*, followed by the emergence of the beautiful golden cage.

The crowd smiled, clapped, and took pictures as three golden retriever puppies and a kitten of an unknown breed came into view. The exact moment Theogad arrived at the edge, the colonel and his soldiers took two coordinated steps back. They aligned themselves next to the CEO of the dog kennel, the leading politicians, and Bishop Claxon.

Theogad involuntarily moved a hand to cover his aching stomach. Mid-move he remembered the television cameras, so he passed over his stomach and straightened his tie instead. He observed how the leaders of his financial, political, and religious systems were lined up, side by side, shoulder to shoulder in solidarity with rows of subordinates behind them. With the cameras rolling, the sky turning from golden to amber, and the crowd growing quiet, Theogad cleared his throat.

"Friends and family of Golden Point and surrounding kingdom. We are a blessed people. And this is a special day."

The cameras panned around the ledge. People from all over the nation saw Bishop Claxon's smile. Then they saw him frown as Theogad continued, "However, we've been misled."

The cameras jerked abruptly back to the king resulting in countless people across the kingdom reaching for solid pieces of furniture to hold onto while steadying their stance.

Theogad's voice grew stronger. "We've been conditioned to think that God isn't happy, and that what He wants is for us to sacrifice these golden retrievers and this kitten."

Theogad looked down at the animals. The cameras followed his gaze. People nationwide watched two of the puppies wrestling, while the other chased its tail around and around. The kitten was curled up in the corner sleeping.

Theogad looked down at them, then at the cameras, then at everyone and said, "We've got this wrong. All wrong. This is ridiculous!"

The crowd lit up, as if a current of electricity had been released from Theogad. It surged outward through the leaders, their entourages behind and the people further back on the cliffs, hanging out the windows, listening down the street, jumping from airplanes, and watching all over the kingdom. The collective jaw of the nation dropped.

What was the king saying?

Theogad continued. "I'm the king. And I've decided we've been in error. I'm not throwing these puppies and kittens off the *cliff*. Why *would* I? God isn't angry. God doesn't need their sacrifice. God isn't upset at us. What kind of God requires the death of little animals in order to accept people?" Theogad shook his head and wrinkled his face as he considered such a question.

"What an insecure God that would be. No, what I think we need to *accept* is how he *already accepts us*! Look at how beautiful this place is. Feel the air." Theogad stretched his hands wide and inhaled deeply. "Smell the food. Hear the ocean breakers. See the richness of relationships around each of us, around the entire kingdom. Can we not see the beauty? Can we not feel his love? Love is what sustains all of this, not fear!" Theogad's voice crescendoed, "We should be serving these animals, not killing them. And in our serving them, we could see the way we serve others. And in all this serving, we could see how God serves us. People of Golden Point"— Theogad paused for effect—"we no longer need to sacrifice animals!"

The king stood still, full of conviction, resolute as the kingdom struggled to breathe. Then, from within the vacuum of noise, a commotion erupted. The colonel, surrounded by his guard, moved to Theogad's side. He took one glance at the bishop and without hesitation picked the king up, calculated the angles, took two steps, and flung him off the cliff. He used optimal trajectory, ensuring four boulders and/or otherwise sharp objects were hit on the way to the king's death in the bay.

The people could only watch. Some grabbed neighbors' arms in shock, some covered their foreheads in confusion. A certain paralysis seized the nation. People were unable to process what they had just witnessed, to close their gaping mouths.

Back at the ledge a moment of silence was chased down by a cry of protest. Some began shouting and moving toward the colonel. Soldiers quickly formed a circle and aimed their rifles outward. The crowd sputtered, lurched, then stopped. No one knew what to do. The entire nation seemed to splinter, convulse, then stand still.

Finally, Bishop Claxon emerged from the milieu. He walked to the ledge, slowly peered over, then turned around and raised his arms toward the people, toward the heavens, but mostly toward the cameras. He commanded everyone's attention. At no point in the history of the kingdom did anyone ever have a more captive audience.

The soldiers took small steps backward, eyes darting left and right. A few began to lower their guns, then reach out and force the barrels of others' guns down as well. The politicians began to straighten jackets and ties, shoulders and spines. The small crowd protesting began to drop arms to their sides and unclench their fists. The nation's limbic system began powering down.

Bishop Claxon's hands spread outward toward the people. He had a tear in his eye. When he spoke, the inflection of his short sentences went from high to low. It gave the effect of a sob, a rhythmic lament.

"Oh, my Golden Point people," he said, shaking his head.

"Oh, my people around the kingdom." More shaking.

"Oh, what a terrible thing has happened today."

"What a tragedy."

Many began to nod in agreement and bow their heads. The politicians and Kennel Point's board of directors shuffled backward slightly.

A pause, then the slightest change in the timbre of his voice. "We have learned today of the error of our ways."

Then, volume increasing, "It has just been revealed to me that God, indeed, all along, has not needed the immolation of puppies and kittens. How small-minded of us to think this was the case." He looked to the ground and shook his head, "No, what God really needs is *something bigger.*" The bishop raised his chin, his arms, his voice. "What he needs is for us to sacrifice a *human!*"

This was a startling statement, never before considered by the people at large. It took a few seconds, like a wave rippling further and further outward for people to register the truth of Bishop Claxon's words. The news gained momentum and traveled further as confusion transitioned into joy. Little by little, people gained clarity, which manifested itself into slaps on backs, then hand claps, then applause. It ebbed and flowed into waves of cheering and celebration out to the furthest regions of the kingdom, then flowed back through the people and back onto the ledge. A great and energetic release of sacrificial unanimity turned into a thunderous ovation.

A minute later, the ovation waning, a few shouts of protest around the ledge could be heard, but they were drowned out by the emboldened bishop. "Yes, this is a blessed day. God is finally showing us how to appease His great wrath. From now on we shall throw *humans* over the ledge." He raised both hands. "This is a time for celebration!"

Another wave of optimism swept the nation, larger than the first. People jumped, clapped, and danced. It wasn't until the cameras shifted to their respective news correspondents, panels, and commercials that the bishop let his hands drop, his shoulders and smile too. The colonel and his soldiers promptly joined his side. They encircled the bishop and moved forward, periodically pulling top politicians and kennel administrators inside the circle.

A remnant of citizens attempted to stop the group and ask questions, but the armed guard easily pushed through their weak protests. The entourage left in the same vehicles, in the same seats, and in the same way they had arrived. Minus a king.

The reporters and pundits clamored over each other to offer commentary regarding the "unexpected epiphany," the "amazing revelation," and the "historical transition" playing out right in front of their eyes.

At the top of the hour lights and cameras shut down and staging and production packed up. The trucks and vans arrived to haul everything away. *The Point of Sacrifice and New Beginnings for Everyone* emptied except for a small but growing number of people wandering mindlessly around the point with the leftover confetti that whirled and whizzed around their feet. They gathered to mourn Theogad and the revolutionary act of mercy he had proposed. Some prayed. Some sat with head in hands. Some wiped tears.

Others shook their head in disbelief over how quickly the kingdom had assumed Theogad's act a *requirement* of God's will, rather than a *revealing of* God's heart.

They made calls, sent texts, and attempted to talk with others out on the street, but most of the people in Golden Point were more or less satisfied with the new turn of events. Restaurant owners needed customers to eat, drink, and celebrate. Party planners needed people to attend parades and watch fireworks. Politicians and economists needed stabilization of markets and fan bases. Religious authorities needed tradition and ritualization. And the military did whatever the political, economic, and religious systems demanded anyhow.

Things were a little less clear for those in the dog-and-cat business. The manufacturers and purveyors of kitten trinkets and stuffed-animal puppies were understandably uneasy about the sudden change. They didn't yet see what the bishop, Kennel CEO, and other shrewd businessmen recognized almost immediately: that it was in essence the same business, with the same core values, holding out promise of the same—maybe even more—profits. They needed only to innovate, to transition from animals to humans. There would be some tricky marketing to navigate, of course, but it could be done. The industry could still be prosperous by aligning itself with the kingdom's deep-seated desires.

So, things returned to normal. The community's entertainment committees got the evening's schedule back on track. Musicians began plugging in, tuning up, and playing. Shop and restaurant owners ushered people into their establishments. It was truly an amazing show of solidarity. Everyone pulled together to jumpstart the celebration. The sky lit up with fireworks. *Thumpf-whoosh-pop-POP-pop.* There was singing, dancing, drinking, and laughing. The death of King Theogad became the talk of the kingdom as its people celebrated late into the night, then into the early hours, saying things like, "Wow, God needs the death of humans to be happy. What an extraordinary event."

And, "I always had a feeling we weren't sacrificing enough."

And, "I'm glad we're on *God's* side."

. . . . .

Out on the ledge of *The Point of Sacrifice and New Beginnings for Everyone,* three golden retriever puppies and a kitten snuggled together in a cage, heads resting on paws. They tracked fireworks across the sky for a while, but eventually their eyelids proved too heavy. They closed their eyes as the night sky swallowed the last of the rockets, arcing, flaming, sizzling, and fading.

The Wrong Side of the Tracks

LaDasia grew up on the wrong side of the tracks. Literally. Her dad was a train mechanic, renting a home on the back lot of the train yard.

LaDasia's neighborhood was the clackity-clack of rail joints, the mesmerizing figure eights of coupling rods, and the ever-present fragrance of fuel. Her backyard was a caboose, retired on its side, dirt, weeds, and sunflowers wildly spilling out into a tiny garden. Her home was the grease-stained fingerprints on lemonade glasses, the soapy fragrance of her father lying next to her at bedtime, and the stubble of his kiss tucking her in, even late into her teenage years, whispering, "Sleep tight grease chicken."

Closing her eyes to the lonely sound of the train whistle, LaDasia didn't imagine she was on the wrong side of anything.

The right side of the tracks was a different world,

and for most, a more desirable place to live. The sights were more sightly, the fragrances more fragrant, and the noises less noisy. LaDasia's friends often visited the right side, pulling her along, balancing on old pipes, climbing through rusty fences, and skipping over dilapidated train tracks. They laughed, dreamed, and enumerated lists of ways life would be better if only they could live on the right side.

Crisscrossing thresholds to both worlds, LaDasia couldn't deny life on the other side was different. She saw, felt, and experienced it, but after a few hours on the right side, she often found herself fielding a variety of emotions. Loneliness? Coldness? Judgment? Maybe all the above. Something was lacking on the right side.

Returning home, late at night, the words of her friends assaulting the quietness of the star-filled sky, LaDasia would drift back a few yards, alone in thoughts, attempting to work out the missing link. Sure, the other side was nice. And yes, some even labeled it perfect. But her nose would scrunch up as she considered the word, perfect: clean lines, indefectible cityscapes, and polished assemblages of architecture, people, and pretense. *Was that what it meant to be perfect? Was perfect a thing you could weigh or measure? Was it something you could regiment or standardize?* Maybe her discomfort didn't center around perfection. Maybe her discomfort centered around definitions of perfection.

She continued to accompany her friends most weekends throughout high school and even after graduating. Still, she always looked forward to returning home, to throw on sweats, wrap up her head of curls, and burrow deep into a bevy of pillows. She had little desire to live somewhere other than her chaotic, authentic, imperfect home.

However, one Friday night, LaDasia's desires began to be influenced. Leaping over tracks, hand in hand, laughing, she and her friends met a group of young men. LaDasia, playfully nudged forward by hands in the middle of her back, introduced herself to a kind young gentleman by the name of Emiliano.

She was immediately intrigued by the confident yet humble manner in which Emiliano carried himself. She guessed he came from somewhere important. Her hunch was confirmed as the night unfolded. Emiliano hesitated, changed subjects, and smiled shyly, but eventually revealed his identity: his father owned the trains. All the trains. And the train yard. The *entire* railroad industry.

LaDasia's eyes widened upon hearing the news. She grew quiet, then separated herself from the crowd to sit down. She took a deep breath and attempted to wrap her mind around the fact that Emiliano's father was the single most powerful man in the world.

A minute later, she slapped her legs and jumped up to find her friends. Approaching the group, she recognized

Emiliano in the back of the group, waiting for her. He stood leaning against a streetlamp, hands in pockets, kicking at something in the street.

He wasn't the most handsome man she had ever met. Though as soon as she concluded the thought, it crashed up against the next thought: then again, he wasn't the most unattractive, either. Yes, his nose was a bit sharp and jagged, like the dorsal fin of a battle-tested shark, but there was nothing sharklike about the rest of his appearance or demeanor. His hair was brilliant and black and fell easily across his forehead. His eyes were inviting and deeply almond. And his voice—she'd heard it as she approached—emanated from somewhere generous and expansive.

"Hi, I thought we lost you," he said.

"No, Emiliano," she shook her head, skipping the last step to stand in front of him squarely. She smiled, "I'm not lost."

He nodded slowly and returned her smile.

"C'mon," she said, ducking her head a bit while brushing her shoulder up against his chest. "Let's catch up with the others."

Despite their contrasting backgrounds, the young couple made a connection—that evening and throughout the following week. And the week after that. LaDasia couldn't quite make sense of the relationship. She wasn't particularly insecure about her inconsequential life on *her* side, but she couldn't help but feel a sense of intimidation whenever she contemplated the importance of Emiliano's family on *his* side.

Emiliano, for his part, did nothing to make her feel insecure. He was, in every sense of the word, a gentleman. He was neither pushy nor controlling. He was neither weak nor overbearing. When they spoke of where they came from, he expressed little anxiety. When they imagined where they might be going, he was confident.

The more time they spent together, the more she learned how he held his father in great respect. His father influenced his decisions, his opinions, and his outlook. He did little without first checking in to see how it would affect his dad or the family business. Ultimately this served to make Emiliano even more endearing. LaDasia related well to someone who respected their father. Not surprisingly, the friendship quickly blossomed with signs of romance.

Early one Saturday morning, only a few weeks into the young couple's relationship, LaDasia's father was in his shed hunched over a workbench. His back slowly warmed in the waking sun as he peered through reading glasses at a small mechanical apparatus. An old transistor radio thinly distributed the fat sounds of eras gone by as he hummed along. Coffee grounds and morning dew billowed in and out as if the shed itself were inhaling and exhaling.

Caught up in his work as he was, LaDasia's father failed to notice a large SUV, burnished black and proud, roll up and onto the yard behind him. It covered the entirety of the dirt drive, a portion of the yard, and even spilled back out onto gravel road. LaDasia's father continued to hum, oblivious. Four black suits stepped out of the car. Two flanked the garage. Two quietly approached the mechanic's back still bent over the workbench.

In a soft but serious tone, one of the black suits said, "Excuse me."

LaDasia's dad swiveled his chair. He was so shocked by the dark suits, so taken aback by the titanic SUV sprawled over the front yard, that he froze, speechless, peering above his readers at the scene unfolding before him.

The backdoors of the SUV opened. The mechanic squinted through countless points of sunlight refracting off the vehicle as a figure emerged. Initially, he could only make out a dark shape; then, closer, the shape took the form of a tall man. Closer still, the man became instantly and shockingly recognizable: the owner of the trains, the train yard, and the entire railroad industry!

The railroad magnate ducked just inside the shed. He stood still for a moment and allowed his eyes to adjust. He pulled gloves off and asked, in a voice as deep as a cave, "Are you LaDasia's father?"

LaDasia's father froze. Only his head nodded.

Emliano's father looked him up and down. "Can you speak?"

The mechanic finally gained a measure of control. He sat up straight. "Oh," he said. Then he stood up. Then he wiped his hands on his overalls and said, "Oh, yes. Yes, I can speak. I speak well."

The lines across the railroad owner's forehead grew more pronounced for a moment.

"Uh, sorry," stammered LaDasia's father. "What I mean is, well, I was unaware ..."

Emiliano's father, attempting to breach the world of differences between them, interrupted the stammering by extending his hand. LaDasia's father looked down at the hand, then hesitantly mirrored the movement, shaking for such a long time that the train mogul had to peel his fingers away.

The mechanic quickly resumed stammering while he began searching the shed for a stool to offer his guest. He was processing a hundred different reasons why this man would be here at his home. He wondered if LaDasia had done something wrong. Or if he had done something wrong. He put one hand on the workbench for stability, the speed of his thoughts causing him lightheadedness.

The railroad owner, wiping his hand on a handkerchief supplied by one of the black suits, noticed the mechanic's distress. He said, "There's nothing to worry about. I'm only here because of my son. I assume you are aware of the relationship between our children?"

"Oh, oh, yes, I do."

"Well," continued the tycoon stretching his hand like a game show host to the car behind, "My son has a request to make of you."

On cue, Emiliano stepped out of the back seat of the SUV. The train mechanic shielded his eyes as more sunlight from the movement of the car door blasted into the toolshed. Emiliano stepped past the black suits and ducked inside. He smiled warmly at LaDasia's father.

And then Emiliano uttered the sentence that altered the mechanic's life. "Sir, I would like permission to ask your daughter to marry me."

Confusion gave way to more confusion for LaDasia's father. This was unexpected. He looked at the floor as if he were trying to find a place to hide. Then he looked back up at Emiliano. He stood motionless, again, with his mouth slightly open. Finally, he closed his mouth, held up one finger, and said, "Could I go get LaDasia? I think she might want to see this. Or hear this, or uh, be here."

Both Emiliano and his father nodded.

LaDasia's father rushed out of the shed. A moment later, he retraced his steps, pointing ahead with one hand and behind with the other, "Sorry, I uh …"—he walked across to the other side of the shed—"I went the wrong …" He didn't finish the sentence. He just walked out the other side and went inside the house.

He used one hand to knock on LaDasia's door and the other to scratch the back of his head. Not willing to knock a second time, he slipped into her room and located her head under an avalanche of pillows and blankets. He said, "Uh, honey?"

LaDasia mumbled something unintelligible, then rolled over without opening her eyes.

"Um, Emiliano and his father are here ..."

"Hm, hm, OK."

"Yeah, look, here's the thing, he's asking for your hand in marriage?"

LaDasia grunted and mindlessly poked some tresses back underneath her bandanna. She attempted to open one eye and said, "Daddy, that's hilarious."

Her father, gently sitting down at the foot of her bed, said, "No, *really*, they're outside right *now*."

LaDasia lay still a moment longer, but then her brain processed the tone of her father's voice. Her eyes shot open. "What?"

Her father nodded his head and patted her leg, although after a few pats, they both realized he was actually patting his own leg.

LaDasia stared at her father's nodding and patting, trying to work through what he was saying. Wildly, she sat up on her elbows and snatched at the window blinds. She slowly lifted one eye just high enough to peek outside. At the sight of Emiliano leaning up against the massive SUV, she dove back under her pillows.

Again, she said, "What?"

She kicked the covers off her feet, leaped out of bed, walked partway down the hallway, then stopped. She turned and looked at her dad to confirm she heard him correctly. He nodded yes as she replayed his words over in her mind. Her eyebrows furrowed so deeply that her forehead became half its normal size as she said with even more intensity, "*What?*"

A moment later, she ferociously ripped the bandanna off her head. She leaned over and shook her hair out. She launched a thousand curls up and behind her as she stood up. She spun on her heels and attacked the hallway to the front door. Barely slowing down, eyes still straight ahead, all in one move, she reached into the half bath, grabbed a bottle of mouthwash, and—still walking—took a swig, swung the front door open, and confidently stepped out onto their small, dilapidated porch. Then, after a moment, she chucked the mouthwash behind her into a bush.

"Ah, there you are," Emiliano laughed. "For a moment, I wondered if you would be joining us."

"Hi!" LaDasia blurted out louder than she intended.

She surveyed the front yard. Although she hadn't

previously met Emiliano's father, she instantly recognized him.

He *seemed* nice.

Good grief, his *car* was nice.

His suit was *very* nice.

Suddenly, she thought of the pajamas she was wearing. Still on the little front porch, in one motion, she reached back inside the house, grabbed her father's hoodie hanging on the coatrack, and quickly pulled it over her head.

Emiliano saw her anxiety, rushed up on the porch, and said, "*Hey, hey,* it's OK."

She asked, "What are you doing? Here? Now." She pulled at the sweatshirt, which came down to her knees, "I mean, what is going on?"

Then Emiliano knelt in front of LaDasia. She gasped, took a step back, and put a hand over her mouth. Her father saw the young man kneeling and his daughter's surprise. Instinctively, in an effort to support her, and because he didn't know what else to do, he stepped up and grabbed her other hand. Emiliano paused at her father's unexpected movement, which gave Emiliano's father time to appreciate the gesture of solidarity between father and daughter. Nodding his head in deference, he stepped forward and grabbed Emiliano's open hand as well.

And there, with Emiliano on one knee, one hand extended to LaDasia holding a ring, the other awkwardly holding onto his father's hand, with LaDasia in her hoodie and pajamas, keeping one hand over her mouth while desperately clutching her father's greasy hand with the other, with the four of them crowded on the little porch, with black suits positioned around the home, with a growing number of children peering through the chain-link fence, and neighbors leaning out windows, and the sun rising in the background, Emiliano said, "LaDasia, will you marry me?"

The entire neighborhood inhaled. The world went quiet for a moment. Then LaDasia slowly lowered her hand from her mouth … and … laughed and laughed.

Over and over again, she laughed.

Her father glanced nervously at his daughter, then at the railroad owner, then at Emiliano, then back to his daughter. He nodded slightly, his countenance announcing to all gathered that he found her to be overjoyed.

As LaDasia continued to laugh, his eyes went through the rotation again: his daughter, the owner, Emiliano, back to his daughter. He rocked up on his toes a bit, turning his head slightly to watch her laugh. Then, with LaDasia doubled over in tears, he rocked even higher and began to drum his fingers on the side of his leg. A drop of sweat formed at the edge of his right eyebrow.

LaDasia snorted and laughed even more.

Emiliano was perplexed. His father even more so. Some

of the neighbors shook their heads. Others quickly looked the other way. Children giggled as they peeked through the fence. The only people unaffected were the four black suits.

LaDasia continued to lean over and laugh. One hand held her side while the other clutched desperately at her father. This went on for several seconds. LaDasia's father's hand began to turn white.

Finally, LaDasia calmed down enough to speak. "Oh, my, *my*," she said, looking at her would-be husband. "Oh, Emiliano, this is the sweetest thing anyone has ever done for me. Honestly, I am *completely* overwhelmed and humbled."

She finally let go of her father and knelt in front of Emiliano. She put both hands on his face, inadvertently transferring grease from her father's hand to Emiliano's face. She burst into laughter again but then quickly regained her composure.

She took a big breath and looked at Emiliano. She turned her head slightly in admiration as she exhaled. The fragrance of mouthwash filled the space between them. "Emiliano, thank you so much, but ..."—she was still holding his cheeks—"but I don't think I'm ready for this kind of commitment. Seriously, this is *such* a big decision. I don't think I can say yes. I am *so* sorry."

Emiliano stood up slowly without response. LaDasia, only a beat behind, mirrored his movement and stood up as well. They looked at each other for a moment.

Emiliano's father said, "Did I hear *correctly*?" Emiliano lowered his head and took a slight step back as his father inched forward.

LaDasia faced the owner and said, "Sir, thank you *so* much. This is all *so* very kind. This is all …"—she extended her hand, gesturing toward the car and the black suits—"it's all so nice. This whole thing is *so* nice. And, and the car is *super* large." She swallowed and rubbed her forehead with the sleeves of the sweatshirt that extended well beyond her hands. "And the guys there with their black suits. Very nice. Very, *very* nice …"

Emiliano's father interrupted her by turning his attention toward LaDasia's father. He looked directly into his eyes, "You must understand, my son loves your daughter."

LaDasia's father begin feeling normal for the first time all morning. He felt clarity and even courage. He wanted to return the railroad owner's look squarely, but with the four of them on the little porch, he couldn't quite pull it off. He tried to glare, but he was too far away. So he shuffled his feet forward, reorganizing the space between the four of them. The less room he could find, the more agitated he grew.

Finally, he gave up, stood straight where he was, and said, "I'm very sorry, sir. Maybe the children need some time." He glanced at LaDasia to confirm she was confident, then back at the owner, and said, "I support whatever LaDasia decides."

Again, it was quiet. Then Emiliano's father spoke. He was confident and controlled. "I don't think you understand. He loves your daughter." As he said this, he reached out to put his hand on LaDasia's shoulder, the other hand on his chest. "I do as well, and I have a wonderful plan for her and her life"—he nodded his head backward—"on the *other* side of the tracks."

A moment later, it was Emiliano's turn to step forward. His father, sensing his movement, shuffled backward. LaDasia and her dad adjusted as well. The four of them recalibrated their positions across the creaking and groaning porch. LaDasia and Emiliano were now in the front, with each of the fathers standing behind.

Emiliano said, "Look, LaDasia, I know this is all kind of sudden, but we really need to make a decision." Emiliano glanced around the neighborhood. LaDasia recognized the glance. She realized, for the first time, that Emiliano wasn't particularly excited about being on the wrong side of the tracks. The thought did nothing but confirm her decision. She said, "But, *why*? What's the rush?"

"I ... I can't stay here." He looked down at his feet.

Feeling her face grow warm, she asked, "Why, what's wrong with *here*?"

"My father has somewhere for me to go, but I really

want you to go with me." His voice rose in intensity as he looked up at her and said, "I love you!"

LaDasia, once again sensing how generous the overture was, attempted to lower her emotion. "I know you do, but I'm not ready. And honestly"—she looked around at her neighborhood and her father—"I love it here." She was forced to increase the volume of the sentence as she said, yelling by the the time she said the word, "here," as noise from a train rolling behind the house crashed in and all around them. She shrugged and held her index finger up, wordlessly asking for patience.

Engulfed in the noise, she killed time by glancing at the fence off to the side of the porch. She noted the random grouping of sunflowers growing up and through the chain links at various heights. She looked up, observing the porch light as it convulsed and swayed to the rhythm of the passing train. She looked out over the yard and road. Neighbors leaning out of windows, smiling and talking to one another. She looked at their faces, then the faces of the black suits devoid of reaction, and then the face of Emiliano's father. She observed the way the wrinkles in his forehead faded as the noise of the train faded.

In the wake of silence that followed the last train car, she clutched at Emiliano's hands and repeated herself. "I *love* it here." Then she added, "there are so many good things."

Emiliano bowed his head in submission. He took a step back onto his father's toe, his father wincing only slightly. Then the two of them reshuffled again, which triggered another repositioning by LaDasia and her father.

The railroad tycoon summed it up. "I think it's obvious how much we love you, LaDasia. I have a wonderful plan. It's not to stay here, in this ..." He peered over his shoulder. "Well, it's not to stay here. I'm so excited for my plan to develop and materialize, however ..."—his eyes locked onto LaDasia's father—"if your daughter refuses Emiliano's hand in marriage I will punish her *and* her household."

LaDasia raised a hand over her mouth. Her father wrapped his arms around her shoulder.

Emiliano's father continued. "It's obvious she and you are obsessed with the wrong side of the tracks. But what fellowship does the wrong side have with the right side? Look, we are freely offering you the way out. I hope you know we offer this way because Emiliano loves her, but if she doesn't respond"—his voice lowered—"she, you, and all your family will lose their jobs."

A bolt of energy shot down LaDasia's arms into fists pointed at the ground. She glared at the man out from under an extended brow.

The owner continued. "And you will be left homeless."

LaDasia's father raised his chin and squeezed his daughter tighter.

"And, unfortunately," he said with resignation, "she will be tied to the railroad tracks."

Anger morphed into confusion for LaDasia. She covered her mouth in horror while her father scrunched up one eye, mouthing the word, "*What?*"

Neither Emiliano nor his father acknowledged their reaction. They spun on their heels, stepped off the porch, and marched back to the SUV.

Emiliano's father threw his hand up in the air to accentuate how wasteful it would be if LaDasia made the wrong choice. "Trains will run over her as she is tied to the tracks." Taking a few more steps, then pausing, he said, "Again, and again."

The last steps were the slowest. The black suits opened the back doors of the vehicle. Emiliano quietly got in first, then his father—who, taking one last look back at LaDasia, repeated, "We love you, but the trains will never stop running over you. Again, and again, for years and years."

He looked at his watch. "We'll give you one hour." He jumped into the vehicle as the door slammed behind him. He stuck his cell phone through the open moonroof, waved it, and shouted, "You know where to find us!"

The SUV, too large for the space it was in, lurched forward, leaving tracks in the yard, then backward, knocking over a trash can. The process repeated itself before it finally sped off down the gravel road.

LaDasia and her father stood speechless with the railroad owner's gracious and magnanimous invitation hanging in the air, floating, dissipating like so much dust in the last of the morning's light.

The Hope and Melvin of Humanity

HOPE and Melvin were good humans, really good humans, navigating difficult times. They had a strong marriage, with a child on the way, but Melvin struggled to find work. Hope did what she could part-time to help their ever-expanding ends meet, but her husband's failure to land a real job was birthing serious financial challenges for the young family.

Some of Hope's friends said the problem was Melvin's background, that he chose the wrong internship or graduated from the wrong school. Others said he should try harder because life helps those who help themselves. Still others attributed the whole situation to God's will. Hope graciously listened to the unsolicited input, but she had a pretty good idea it was none of the above.

One evening over cheap wine, laughing, rolling her eyes at some of the trending explanations, she talked with

Melvin late into the night. They sat on the balcony on the back of their little condo, a hill that opened out over a few highways and trees below and a sky full of stars above.

Limbs wrapped up in oversized sweatshirts.
Humans wrapped up in an oversized night sky.

Melvin's finger traced the top of his Solo cup as he said, almost more breathing than speaking, "I wish I could fix this for us."

She looked at him through various shades of evening light. There was worry in his voice, a contrast to his normal easy personality, something so noticeable and attractive years ago in their very first encounter.

Chemistry lab.
Back corner.
Bunson burners.
Laughter.
His warmth. Eighties glasses. Looking like a black Clark Kent.

Hope pulled long, straight, dark hair behind her ear as she leaned into his periphery, "Hey, I know," she said. "This is a lot. Look, there's always going to be challenges, things that hurt. Life is just like that. It can't all be fixed.

It's not your fault. We gotta learn how, *I don't know* ... to carry it well."

A smile from the corners of his mouth influenced the edges of his cheeks up and into his eyes. He settled down into his chair. His glasses shifted with the slightest twitch of his nose, a signal he was listening.

He repeated her phrase as if rearranging it a little, trying it on for size, "Don't fix everything, just carry it well? I'm unsure what it means, but it sounds good."

She tapped his knee with the back of her hand and sat back to stretch her back, to stretch her mind, to consider what it meant to carry things well. Questions, like the stars above, appeared and disappeared.

How do you carry things well without answers?
What do these questions mean?
Why are we going through this?

She began to tear up. "Ah, freaking hormones!"

She snatched a tissue and wiped her nose. Sitting back, she noticed Melvin out of the corner of her eye, grinning. She narrowed her gaze, gunmetal-blue eyes staring at him in mock anger, but then she smiled with him. She reached over in the stillness, grabbed his hand and put it over hers, over the new life to come, and squeezed.

. . . . .

HOPE leaned into their questions. She intended to help her little family figure out how to "carry things well." She prayed, reflected, and read. She had always enjoyed reading, but during this season she was intentional about reading the Bible.

She was full of questions as she read, at times in an eye of a storm, relaxed and giving herself room to challenge presuppositions, and at other times, at the forward edge, winded, chasing down clarity.

One Saturday night, fatigued from chasing, she gently tossed her Bible aside and asked Melvin his thoughts about attending church. Before he answered, Hope clicked on a church website and noticed a new ten-week sermon series, beginning the next day, titled "Finding Answers During Difficult Times."

"This could be helpful, right?" She continued reading but held her palm up to elicit feedback. Melvin, on the couch next to her, smiled and gave her a high five.

They showed up early the following day and gave themselves a short self-guided tour of the building, noting the nursery and children's area. A few people smiled as they walked into and down to the front of the auditorium. Not the first row. "Obviously," she whispered, "that'd be weird." Then she pointed to the second row.

In time, as screens full of countdowns reached zero, fading into shifting, ethereal visuals, a young man appeared on stage. He walked from behind dark, billowing drapes into a soft spotlight. He greeted people over the sounds of evolving pedal tones and guitar pads, then led everyone in a heartfelt prayer, the *amen* triggering a light change and a fury of sounds.

Hope leaned back, wide-eyed, as the band led the auditorium through a passionate series of high-tempo, drum-looped songs and evocative keyboard-driven ballads. Powerful and beautiful energy filled the room. Hope started to close her eyes and absorb the moment but then noticed that what the vocalists wore matched what the band wore. And matched the drapes, background, and graphics.

She lost a few seconds glancing over at what Melvin wore, then down at what she wore. She stole a look at the people around them in the auditorium. Had she missed something? Was there an announcement online she should've noticed? She worked through a progression of feelings for about half a song but then collected herself with a shake of her head. She recentered herself with a big breath and recommitment to be in the moment.

They listened to the announcements, laughed at a video, downloaded a church app, and gave some money. Then as lights and music brightened, they were invited to greet others. The regulars began milling about the auditorium. Hope and Melvin remained seated for a moment, then stood slowly. She looked up at him, widened her eyes, and leaned up on her toes to give him a shoulder bump. Melvin reciprocated.

A second later, someone tapped Hope's shoulder. Hope turned and recognized a lady she'd seen on the screen earlier, or in the bulletin, or a picture in the foyer, or maybe it was in a magazine: tall, a bit older, capable, surely in charge of something.

"Hi, my name is Jan."

Jan wore an oversized lapel coat, midlength, beige, single row of buttons, wide lapels, belted across the middle.

"Oh, hello," Hope responded, taken back by Jan's friendliness, her panache, *good grief, her teeth.* Jan had the most beautiful smile Hope had ever seen.

"Welcome," Jan said, followed by, "Is this your first time?" Then, "How'd you hear about the church?"

Hope attempted to respond but was distracted by her own reflection in the ivory gleam. She started to peer in to check her hair, but then Jan asked, "Would you like me to introduce you to a few people?"

"Oh …," Hope drew her response out, her arm raising as if reaching for the pull-cord on a bus. But then she opened her hand and said, "Yes! Let's do it."

She followed Jan out into the aisle and the furthest reaches of the auditorium, laughing at her sudden popularity, Jan's prodigious smile parting groups of people like Moses and his staff parting the Red Sea.

As the greeting time drew to a close, Hope headed back to her seat. She watched Melvin make his way over to someone and extend his hand at the exact moment the lights and sound changed. It was a cue for regulars to scurry back to their positions. She stifled a laugh as Melvin left his hand outstretched toward the back of a retreating man only to clasp his left hand over the right, then, with a slow-motion nod, take steps backward to his seat.

Hope caught up with him, put her hands over his, and whispered, "Smooth." They both laughed as lights and sound continued to shift and morph. They were in the dark by the time they found their row. They leaned over and located their seat more by feeling than looking as the pastor emerged from billowing curtains.

Hope watched him stroll to the podium, shoulders back, moving in a way that indicated he knew how to get things done. He was taller than anyone who had yet to be on stage, older as well. He had a substantial head of hair, perhaps jet-black in his youth but now peppered with age, that shot fountainlike up and behind him into the firmament. He reached his destination a full three seconds before his hair.

He paused, placed both hands on either side of the podium, allowing the gravitational pull of the room to reach its full effect, swirl, then settle with a bevy of production lights highlighting a billion dust particles in genuflection.

He leaned back to scan the crowd. Hope held her breath momentarily, fearing the weight of his hair would pull him over backward. But he stood straight, scanned the crowd, then began.

His first sentence was heavy, abrupt, but careful, like the downbeat of a padded sledgehammer. The room resonated.

Hope unsheathed her pen, bit her lip, and leaned forward. Melvin smiled at her and said, "Here we go."

Following the service, Jan walked her into the foyer and introduced her to a group of ladies. A pack of children ran in and around their legs as the moms talked and smiled.

All things considered, Hope enjoyed the experience. "The sermon was a little intimidating," she commented on the way home, "but I liked some of the gals I got to meet. I think I could see myself hanging out with them."

. . . . .

THEY showed up a second Sunday repeating the exercise. Hope reconnected with Jan and some of the ladies during the greeting time while Melvin carefully triangulated his position between people, lights, and seats.

Preparing for the pastor's entrance, Hope pulled out her bulletin from the previous week's sermon and reacquainted herself with her notes and scribbles sprawling out to the edges of the page. She studied it, tapped a pen on her chin, turned the bulletin sideways to note the main points she'd circled: *chasms, bridges,* and *sin._*

And then she filled her bulletin again as well as an offering envelope. She wrote, nodded, nudged Melvin a time or two, and underlined the importance of *guilt, bloodshed,* and *forgiveness.*

They repeated the process in weeks three, four, and five, Hope furiously writing on bulletins, offering envelopes, gum wrappers, old receipts from the bottom of her purse. She rubbed her forehead, bounced her knee, and glanced at Melvin as she traced and retraced the pastor's emphasis on *obedience, sacrifice,* and *suffering.*

One Sunday, when everything within arm's reach was already full of outlines, charts, and scratches, she reached to write on the back of her arm but stopped when Melvin poked her and shook his head. She started to protest but then smiled as he whispered through the side of his mouth in a calculated tone, "Please back away from the pen."

Hope took a breath, sat back, exhaled, and attempted to refocus. She pursed her lips and tapped her leg to the rhythm of a growing uneasiness. Then pulled her hair behind her ears to give her a chance to scan the auditorium.

What are others going through?
What difficulties are they experiencing?
Are they suffering?

She glanced at a couple roughly their age on the other side of the aisle but then caught herself looking for evidence that they were taking notes. Embarrassed, she quickly settled back into her chair and willed concentration. She did her best to refocus on the pastor, great dogmatic waves of hair swaying systematically in the light, but she just couldn't recapture her initial excitement. She folded her arms over her midsection and a growing sense of doubt and frustration about what they might be experiencing.

. . . . .

BACK home, the bills were growing.

Hope's body was growing.

And Melvin's frustrations over a lack of a job were growing.

It wasn't the easiest of times.

But one morning, Melvin spotted an email with the subject line *Massive conglomeration of a company that accounts for half of all innovations and revenue of the world's tech industry has openings for positions in management.* Melvin opened the email and realized it was SuperTech. He leaned back and yelled, "Hope, SuperTech is hiring!"

"Who are they again?"

"You know, it's that massive conglomeration of a company

that accounts for half of all innovations and revenue of the world's tech industry!"

"Okay, then, sounds impressive." She clapped him on the back as she walked by with a load of laundry, smiling. "Let's go, let's go!"

Melvin rushed straight to the SuperTech complex. He was first in line and, as it turned out, first in impressions. He hit a home run, and SuperTech hired him on the spot.

Melvin raced home and into the driveway, throwing the car in park while opening the door. He was in such a hurry he burned a handful of hairs off his head skimming it across the rubber sealer of the car door. He barely noticed, busy as he was taking five steps where it usually took ten to cover the distance to the front door. He dropped his backpack in the hallway, loosened his tie, and found Hope pointing the remote at the TV with one hand and holding the phone to her ear with the other. He kissed her on the cheek.

She lowered the phone for a moment, whispering, "It's Jan, from church." Melvin nodded, then threw his suit jacket over the couch on his way to the kitchen.

"Thank you, yes …," Hope said into the phone. "That's kind. Yes, I'm feeling well." She glanced down at her growing stomach.

Melvin searched back to the furthest corners of the fridge to find something celebratory to drink.

Hope continued: "Okay," and "Mm-hmm," and "Thank you," then, "Yes, of course, we'll see you Sunday. Thank you again."

Melvin spun toward her as he heard her finish the conversation. She walked into the kitchen, pace slowing, as Melvin finished his spin holding two juice boxes. She paused and tilted her head.

"It's all we have to celebrate," he said, the volume of his sentence increasing as he continued, "because someone just landed a *new job!*"

He leaped across the kitchen to pick her up but remembered she was heavier than she'd previously been. He stifled a grunt and set her down swiftly but gently. They laughed as he handed her a juice box and they clunked the bottom edges together.

"Cheers," the one said after the other.

Hope took a long draw on the juice box and nodded. "Okay, okay," she said, "maybe it's a new day for Hope and Melvin."

. . . . .

THE couple soldiered through more of the sermon series, although their seating location changed weekly. They sat on the far-right side of the auditorium on week seven, halfway up, and listened to the message titled, "GRATITUDE: You

Deserve Punishment, Not Answers to Prayer."

They slid back a few more seats by week nine when the title of the sermon was, "PEACE: Harmony Between Mind and Body is Antithetical to Christianity."

Following the service, Hope caught up with Jan and a few of her new acquaintances. The group pinged a variety of topics back and forth, sometimes one at a time, sometimes all together. It was like a well-coordinated game of table tennis between seven ladies playing simultaneously.

Parenting and work,
gardening and children,
Bible studies and politics.

Well-coordinated—until Hope spoke to a friend next to her about an incident that had taken place in her yoga class the previous week.

Suddenly the energy of the conversation around her changed. She felt the ping-pong balls of topics bouncing away, but she continued talking, attempting to scan faces and interpret body language. By the time she realized that yoga was considered an "un-Biblical" practice, the silence was firmly entrenched.

One of the ladies began pressing wrinkles out of her skirt, another took a protracted drink of coffee, another hummed and stared at the ceiling. Jan grew quiet and smiled as Hope's excitement about what took place in the yoga class went from enthusiastic to mumbling in the span of one or two sentences. Hope rubbed her forehead and attempted a joke, but by then, Jan was hugging her as others patted her back and walked away. She stood, arms at her sides, allowing Jan to embrace her as she craned her neck, looking for Melvin.

Jan backed up but kept both hands extended to rub Hope's arms for a second. Then she reached over and pulled the top of Hope's bulletin out of her purse far enough to draw attention to the morning's sermon all of them had just experienced. Hope looked down and was reminded of the subtitle: "Harmony Between Mind and Body is Antithetical to Christianity."

"What? Wait." She held her hands out. "Yoga is antithetical to Christianity? How can that be?" Her face was flushed as she looked over Jan's shoulder at the ladies walking away. "Where are they going?"

Jan winced a little as she looked at the foyer emptying then back at Hope. "Sorry, Hope. That didn't go well."

Hope crossed her arms.
Straightened her shoulders.
Slightest flare of an already imperious nose.

"There's no good explanation for how everyone just acted

there, but there is an explanation on how the church views things like yoga and meditation …,"—Jan took a breath—"and you know, other 'new-age type' practices. You may have to relisten to the sermon"—she pointed at Hope's sermon notes again—"but basically it has to do with original sin, how the body, you know, the flesh, is corrupted. Therefore, the church is, well, reluctant to trust anything that kind of emphasizes or highlights the body and bodily movements."

Hope shifted her weight. "So, the body is bad?"

"Well, no, I mean, yes, the church believes the body is sinful."

"Is that what *you* believe?"

"I don't know, I mean, the Bible does teach that we're all sinners, that we've fallen short of God's glory, that the sinful passions are at work in our flesh to bear fruit for death."

"But Jan, why would God intentionally create something bad?"

"Well, I'm not sure he intentionally created something *bad*." She repeated Hope's phrase slowly, looking at the floor then back at Hope. "What he created was good, but it's just that sin messed everything up."

"But why is there sin in the first place?" Hope asked.

"Well, it seems that in his love, God permits sin to enter the world. He hates it. But he decides that what he hates will come to pass."

Hope tilted her head slightly. She shifted her purse to her other shoulder.

He decides that what he hates will come to pass?

Jan seemed to read her countenance and rushed to explain. "It isn't wrong for God to will that there be sin. He's God. He can do whatever he wants. We don't need to worry ourselves over what he does."

"But I kinda *do* worry about his actions," Hope said.

"Oh, I don't think you need to," Jan responded genuinely. "I mean we could be content, as we think about sin, in thinking about Joseph and his brothers. After his own brothers sold Joseph into slavery, he said to them …,"—she paused and then quoted the passage—"'As for you, you meant evil against me, but God meant it for good.'"

Hope's nose scrunched slightly, "But Joseph was talking to his brothers, right? Not to *God*. Doesn't the whole thing change if God, who we believe to be good …,"—she paused—"and full of love …,"—paused again—"is the one who wills bad things?" She held her hands up in the air. "How could one be called a good parent if they intentionally allowed bad things into their child's life?"

Jan turned and put her arm around Hope as they began to walk to the parking lot. "His ways are higher than our ways, Hope. We just can't always see it." Jan's voice grew softer. "Even though bad things are happening, he's still capable and in control."

Hope wasn't a big fan of control. She'd never met a controlling human she enjoyed being around. *Why would God have to be controlling?*

Hope noticed Melvin walking her way. She raised her chin to gain his attention, then cinched her arms inside of his when he got close. Jan took a step away and looked at Hope. "Look …," Jan said, shrugging, "I'm really sorry about how that all played out, Hope. Please forgive them. Forgive me."

Hope relaxed a little. Her face was no longer flushed. She nodded and squinted her eyes. "Yeah, that was unfortunate."

"If you don't want to, it's okay, but do you think we could get together and talk more about it?"

"Maybe," Hope replied. Then, "I'll think about it."

They walked to the car as Melvin asked about the conversation. She frowned. Sighed. But then ducked her head and shoulder-bumped him, covering a laugh. Then she launched into the details. Hand waving, eyebrow arching, sometimes laughing, sometimes cursing, all the way home.

· · · · ·

THE following Sunday morning, they lay on their bed blinking at the ceiling fan. It was the last Sunday of the ten-week sermon series.

Hope asked, "Do you think it means we've lost all faith if we don't go?"

He replied, "Nah, but I might lose all faith if we *keep* going."

Hope laughed, "You might be right."

A few fan rotations later: "Do you believe in hell?"

"I don't know." Melvin put a pillow behind his head, "I think what I believe in is God."

A minute later, she threw her covers off, sat up, collected herself, and walked into the living room. It was, at that point, too late to physically get to the church on time. She made a coffee, opened her laptop, and clicked the link to watch the conclusion to the series online, the message titled, "SUFFERING: It Was God's Answer for Jesus, and It's God's Answer for You."

Hope didn't take any notes during the final sermon. She spent most of her time in the corner of her couch, twisting her mouth, biting her lip, mindlessly circling the word SUFFERING on scrap paper. Partway through, she scribbled out the sentence, "Why did God's son have to die?" Then she drew an arrow from the word SUFFERING to the question. In the act of tracing over the arrow, back and forth, side to side, a deeper and deeper shade of blue, a memory materialized.

Age sixteen or seventeen. She had been seeing a boy for a few months.

What was his name? Harry? No, Harris. Yes. Harris, shirt always buttoned to the neck as if hiding something.

She tried to picture his face but couldn't quite put it together, though she vividly remembered the dozen red roses he unexpectedly gifted her one evening. It was, as he said, *an act of pure love.*

Flowers extended.
He had one leg on the broken steps of the front porch.
She had one leg holding the screen door open.
Her hands reaching out, awkwardly accepting the gift.

She rolled her eyes, thinking about the moment, her naïveté, her assumption that they were, in fact, a gift given *freely.* The flowers proved to be nothing more than currency used to initiate a transaction, a particular transaction that turned out to be even more awkward than the exchange on her front porch.

She thought about transactions.
Freedom.
Love ... what it means to give oneself away.

She lobbed a curse word or two back in her memory, toward Harris, toward that season in her life.
But then, as if breathing in the entirety of that clumsy

and graceless event, she inhaled for a second, or two, or three. And in an act of forgiveness, she exhaled.

She closed her laptop before the service even concluded. She pulled out her phone and located Jan's number. She paused, tapping the phone against her chin a few times. But then she began typing. She got a few words in, started over, retyped, then hit *send*.

. . . . .

LATER that week, Hope greeted Jan at their front door with a quick hug and a handshake. They chatted momentarily, then walked her through the living area and out to the balcony. Jan placed a box of cookies onto the coffee table.

"Yes!" Hope said, raising both her fists.

Jan strolled out to the railing. She wore long dark jeans covered by a buttoned tunic sweater the color of smoke and silver, not unlike the evening sky all around them. She took a deep breath as she wrapped the sweater around her shoulders.

Hope rearranged three wicker chairs to face the sunset, turned some pillows over, and sat down. She was ready to get straight to the point, but she also wanted to be gracious with her friend and the cookies she brought, which, unfortunately, turned out to be drier than expected. They fought through the dehydration with unintelligible noises, fingers held in the air to ask for a moment, multiple glasses of water. They watched dusk turn to twilight as they attempted to recalibrate moisture levels in their mouths.

Finally, after her third glass of water, Hope said, "Jan, thanks for coming over. I want to be respectful"—she moved the empty glass on the coffee table over a few inches and then back again—"but can I just ask a few things?"

"Of course." Jan smiled. "I was happy to get your text. I didn't know if I'd ever see you again after the, well, the horrible way that conversation went down a few weeks ago in the foyer."

Hope shook her head. "It's okay, I've got bigger things on my mind." She patted her legs as if to jump-start her question. "Okay, sorry, but why *crucifixion*? Why did God's son need to die?"

Jan widened her eyes for just a moment, "Yes, let's start with something easy." She took a breath. "I'm not a theologian, but I think he had to die, well, because there is no forgiveness without the shedding of blood."

"But *why*? Why would blood need to be shed?"

Jan pulled the sweater around her shoulders tighter. "Blood signifies life. Nothing happens without blood. It's a representation of how serious all of this sin is."

Hope closed her eyes momentarily, then approached the question from another angle. "And the blood of Christ needed to be shed *because* …?"

"Because only the blood from a perfect sacrifice could actually deal with our sin. The blood of bulls and goats couldn't cover our indiscretions. It was only his blood."

"So, can God forgive without his son dying?"

"Well ...,"—Jan twisted her mouth slightly—"no, ultimately, I don't believe he can. Someone or something needs to pay for the damages done."

Hope negotiated with a pillow to find a more comfortable position. "But, if God needs to be paid, how is it forgiveness?"

"What do you mean?" Jan asked, taking a sip of water.

"I mean, how can you call something forgiveness if it isn't given freely? Is love transactional, or is it *free?* How can you pay for *forgiveness?*"

"Well ...," Jan said slowly, looking up, her eyes following the roof of the balcony to the furthest corner. "I guess in this instance, the way it works is that it's God who's the one paying." She stared more intently into the corner, "And if he's the one paying, *he* gets to set the terms."

"And the terms were that God needed to kill his own son to feel better about *forgiving?*"

"Uh ...,"—Jan closed one eye—"I never thought about it that way before." She scratched her ear for a moment, then said, "I don't think it made God feel better, *necessarily,* but yes, I think it was God's will that his son would die." She took a breath, smoothed her sweater out over her legs, and tucked it under her knees as if putting that part of the conversation behind them, "But he *had* to do this, Hope. Evil is serious. I mean, obviously, it's serious. But I think the point is, it can only be forgiven by a very serious act.

"Would a judge be good if he ... let's say, let a murderer go free ... without demanding some kind of verdict for the victim's family? Would you call that good? I don't think so. God just couldn't sweep our sins under the carpet." She crossed her arms, leaned toward the evening sky, and said, "For the gift of salvation to be given us, God's wrath needs to go *somewhere*."

Hope shifted in her chair and followed Jan's gaze out into the sky.

Does God's wrath need to go somewhere?

She fixed on a distant and sparkling star. She had more questions, but her body needed a change of position. She stood with hands over her stomach and stretched her back.

Jan looked at her and smiled. "Everyone doing okay in there?"

"Yes," Hope responded. "I think the baby is asking questions too."

"You know, I think that's my cue to keep moving. I appreciate the invite. And I *really* appreciate all the water." She leaned forward to locate her purse. "I'll try and find something a little less dry next time!"

She stood and waited for Hope to finish stretching. Then

they walked inside, Hope following her into the living room, as Jan looked back and said, "I hope this helped. We should do this again." And into the front hallway: "You have some really difficult questions." And then, after a quick hug in the doorway: "Keep believing, Hope. Don't lose faith."

· · · · ·

THE following week Melvin started with SuperTech. He arrived early on a Monday morning. Administrative help ushered him into a bustling boardroom full of interns and attorneys.

Someone pulled a chair out for him at the end of a large conference table. The other end of the table stretched out to a window at the far end of the room. It provided a stunning view of the SuperTech complex, and further out, the golden foothills being lit up by the rising sun.

Melvin peered out for only a moment. His view was suddenly obstructed with a thud of documents and a thin whack of a pen. It was deposited by an administrative assistant in a business suit the color of wet leaves and concrete. After dropping the pile of papers, she rotated a plant, wiped at a piece of microscopic lint on a credenza, then walked around the table, attempting to make each chair as straight as her own posture.

When she returned, Melvin leaned back in his seat with an eyebrow and finger lifted. He started to ask a question, but someone walked into the room, nodded at the pile of papers, cell phone pulled down long enough to say, "Legal stuff, Melvin. Just some standard documents, contracts, disclosures, stuff like that."

The man left as quickly as he'd entered. The rest of the room filled up with SuperTech employees. Then Melvin dove into the pile, furiously signing, checking, and initialing amid the chatter of weekend parties and ball-game scores. The further into the pile, the more his pace slowed. The more his pace slowed, the more the chatter around the room slowed. By the time Melvin reached the last page, the place was quiet. He pored over every sentence.

"Everything okay?" he was asked by someone in an expensive suit with blades like white collars. There wasn't time to respond. "You know, there's nothing to worry about. We require all our employees to sign disclosures. It's kinda like a prenup. We hope to be in a long-term relationship, Melvin. We just have to make sure that trade secrets aren't revealed."

Melvin kept going, initialing and signing all but the last box and line. His pen hovered over the page.

"Melvin," a crisp navy blazer said, back turned to Melvin, gazing out the window, "what you'll be working on is strictly proprietary. We need to be able to trust our employees."

A pause. Then, "Melvin, you are trustworthy, right?"

Melvin's eyes darted around the room again. He raised his pen slightly as the room inhaled. Finally, he dropped his hand to check the last box and provide the last signature.

· · · · ·

AT Jan's request, Hope met up with her for coffee a week or two later. They walked into a local café together, Jan collecting glances like a magnet collecting paperclips.

They found a spot in the front corner, by the window, where the dark Koa wood of the window frame met up with brick-and-mortar wall. The late morning sun angled in across their table and throughout the room as the espresso machine provided background music.

Hope and all nine months of her expectation squeezed into the corner seat. She had to move the table to fit, which caused it to shriek across the concrete, eliciting cringes from several patrons.

Jan immediately reached to help, but unfortunately, her chair shrieked even louder than the table as she moved. They both froze. It was only a split second, but in the awkward wake of the noise, an elderly lady rubbing her ear let out a string of profanity.

Both Jan and Hope burst into laughter as the ambiance

of the room convulsed then normalized. Jan laid her head over on her still outstretched arms, shoulders shaking. Hope did her best to melt into the corner. She laughed, swiped at a tear, and tried to keep her bladder from feeling all the pressure.

The ladies replayed the clumsy sequence two or three times between hand motions, laughter, and groans. Somewhere in the middle of all the commotion, the embarrassment, the humanity … Hope decided she liked Jan. She didn't formulate that exact sentence in her mind, it was just a natural movement, like the sun moving slowly across the sky outside the picture window, but that's the conclusion she reached.

"Jan, what's your story? Why are you here? I mean, not necessarily why are you here now with me, but, you know, *here*."

Jan smiled and tapped a rhythm with fingers, muted to clicked, fingertips to curved almond nails.

She repeated the question, "Why am I here?" She looked out the window, then back at Hope, and said, "Well, I'm here, today with you, because … honestly, Hope, the questions you asked a few weeks ago lodged into my mind, or heart, or *something*." She shook her head slightly. "And it's just stirred up a lot of stuff."

"Sorry."

"You don't have anything to be sorry about," Jan replied,

turning the cup in her hands. "But in my world, Hope, questions aren't exactly welcomed."

"Your world?"

"Yeah, my world—the church," Jan said slowly.

Then she picked up the tempo, "Okay, here's the deal. Born and raised in the church. Worked in the church. Only wanted my entire life to please God. Married at a young age. Had a late-term miscarriage. And then another. And, well …,"—one hand clasped the side of the table as if reaching for support—"in the aftermath, I found myself single. Neither a mom nor a wife." She stopped suddenly. The sentence lurched then stalled, like someone learning how to drive a stick shift.

In the wake of the moment, Hope reached out and put her hand over Jan's. Jan relaxed her grip, then reciprocated with a couple of quick squeezes.

Both ladies sighed.

"I know. It's a lot, and it's okay—we don't need to get into all of it. Thank you very much for asking, but your questions reminded me of all my questions that *apparently* …,"—she shifted—"that apparently, I still have."

Hope watched her for a moment, smiled warmly, and said, "I need names. Did the babies have names?"

Jan breathed a slow smile, "Yes. Mia and Penelope."

"Oh gosh, *Mia and Penelope?*"

Jan nodded her head, whispering each of their names

again in confirmation as if reminding the universe of their existence.

"I love those names," Hope said.

A cloud of memories traveled across Jan's face.

"Thank you for asking." Jan turned her head for a moment to form another sentence, but then she stopped abruptly, sighed, and said again, "Thank you." Then, "So yes, I have questions."

"Questions like …?"

"Questions like …," She scanned the room, then lowered her voice. "If God is in control, then why has my life turned out this way?

"And not just me," she quickly added. "Why is there so much suffering?"

Hope nodded.

Jan looked down at her shoes, "I know what I've been taught. That bad things happen because we live in a fallen world." Jan's body movements worked through an answer. "When Adam and Eve sinned, it started this chain of reactions that wreaked havoc on everything."

Hope chimed in, "But if God controls, if he knows what's going to happen beforehand, if he knew the plan from the beginning, how is it Adam and Eve's fault? *Or any of us?*"

Jan nodded and grimaced at the same time. "Yeah." And then, "You know, I do think we still have a response." She tapped her coffee mug lightly against the table. "I mean, we still have choices to make."

"But, if God already knows everything that's going to happen, how is it a choice on our part?"

Jan looked out the window. "I just know the Christian tradition tells us God's aware of what's going to happen and what we're going to do." She nodded her headed slightly with each point. "But it also tells us he isn't responsible for our choices. So bad things happen, yes, but God still must be in control."

Hope looked Jan in the eye and said, "I understand bad things happen. That's life. What I don't understand is why a loving God, knowing that bad things are going to happen, still allows them. Why? Does he *need* the bad?"

"Oh, I don't think God needs *anything*." Jan crossed her arms. "No, God doesn't need anything. He's happy no matter what. His emotions aren't swayed by us or anything."

As she talked about a controlled and unaffected God, a breeze seemed to pass through their conversation. Hope squared her shoulders, leaned into the breeze, and brought the entirety of herself to bear against the changing winds.

She said slowly, "I don't know everything, but I've always had the sense that if a God exists, he's surely a God of love. And …,"—she drew an imaginary circle on the table and tapped her fingers to the beat of the rest of her sentence— "that he loves me."

She paused for a moment, then—over a few inches, making another circle—she said, "What I have learned is that the church *talks* about love. But what it's talking about ...?"—she tapped inside the second circle—"doesn't appear to be the same love ...,"—she moved her hand back to the first—"as *this* love."

Jan grew quiet and listened.

"*This* ...,"—Hope pointed to the first circle—"doesn't feel like it can be purchased or bought." She searched for another way to say it. "It doesn't feel like it can be swayed by behavior or performance.

"But *this*?" Her forehead wrinkled as her hand moved again. "It feels very conditional. Conditioned upon my belief, my mental ascent, my response, my behavior, my ...,"—she paused for a moment—"my sacrifice, or *someone's* sacrifice, and after a while? It just kinda feels like coercion."

Jan twirled the plastic stirrer around the bottom of her empty coffee cup. She went around one way several times, then reversed direction, saying, "I don't disagree. I just ...,"—she paused and started again—"I just don't know how to explain to people when the Bible is so clear about, I don't know, I guess, about judgment."

"I don't get it either, Jan. Like, why are we instructed to love and forgive, but God doesn't have to?"

"What do you mean?"

"Why does he get to send some people to hell—no, most

people ...,"—Hope edited her sentence—"because the path to destruction, according to the Bible, is wide, right?" She waited for Jan to nod, then continued, "Then why does he get to send most people to hell without forgiving them while simultaneously demanding that we forgive? Why does he ask us to do something *he's* not willing to do?"

Jan closed one eye to concentrate. She shifted forward and drummed her fingers. She looked out the window. "Oh, gosh, I don't know. Why *is* that the case? I know what the church has said, basically that we just have to be content with God's choices."

Hope watched Jan's shoulders tighten. "Is that what you feel right now? Contentment?"

They both sat in silence.

Four or five teenagers walked by on the sidewalk in front of them, right to left. Hope took a drink of tea and watched them through the window. A handful of leaves laughed in and around their feet, swirling. Shoulder to shoulder, turning, waving: a murmuration of joy sweeping across their view.

One day her child would be a teenager. If what the church taught was true—that someone could suffer divine punishment for eternity unless they prayed the right prayer, in the right way, at the right time—it would be better to abort her child than to give birth. *Why take a chance that the child could wind up in hell?*

She put both hands over her stomach and felt a hot flash. *If God is merciful to unborn children—something the church generally believes—it would make more sense to have an abortion than to give birth.*

Of course, that would send her to hell because abortion was a sin, but as she sat in the café that morning, feeling the baby moving inside of her, she knew her choice. *If it meant I'd have to go to hell to save my child? I would do it.*

She shook her head slowly over the absurdity of such a predicament.

· · · · ·

MELVIN dove into the job at SuperTech, but unfortunately, it didn't take long for him to figure out why he'd been asked to sign the "prenup." SuperTech, that leading global company, that flagship of capitalism's enterprise, that shining example of all a corporation could become, was engaged in unethical business practices.

Specifically, Melvin's department—Product Development—was responsible for disposing old product. Because you can't have new product with old product lying around. SuperTech had developed a unique and proprietary way to dispose of chips, circuit boards, cables, phones, and gaming systems. Or at least they *labeled* their product-disposal method as unique and proprietary, but it was the same thing all the other tech companies did: they exported their waste to another country. The trash of the global north was being dumped onto the shores of the global south.

On more than one occasion, Melvin had imagined what time-lapsed footage of a Caribbean beach moving from unspoiled to landfill might look like. Or a South American rainforest morphing into a hazardous-waste site. Or a nine-year-old American boy unpacking a new gaming system, while a nine-year-old Haitian boy, running through a trash dump that was previously a grove of banana trees, sliced his foot on an old gaming system.

Melvin wasn't anti-technology; he was a tech enthusiast. He wasn't ungrateful for his job; he was thankful to provide for his family. But the more SuperTech's practices became apparent, the more uneasy he grew.

What role was his country playing?
What role was SuperTech playing?
What role did he play?

So, the months slowly filled with guilt and conviction, frustration and stress.

However, there were some very good events—like, for example, a new baby boy. Melvin and Hope named him Samuel. His addition introduced much joy into their lives. They commented on how crazy it was that their lives had been turned upside by the little guy—but how much they *loved* that their lives had been turned upside down by the little guy.

In the mornings, they played with him, kissing his neck, taking turns passing him back and forth in laughter. In the evenings, after he began walking, they chased him up and down the neighborhood. On the weekends, they elbowed each other quietly and pointed across the room when he was doing something new, like mimicking a baseball player's swing on TV.

They played rock, paper, scissors to see who would put him to sleep at night, at least until Melvin went on a particularly good stretch and won five nights in a row. Then Hope changed the game. But, yes, Samuel was undoubtedly a blessing.

There were other positive things, too, like the people who started hanging out with Melvin. They often said things like, "I'm so proud of how you turned things around," as they swung fists across their chest. Some of their religious friends said, "Isn't God good? He's obviously blessing you."

So they had that going for them.

And of course, Melvin was making good money, more money than he'd ever dreamed. Unfortunately, the paychecks came barnacled with anxiety and guilt about the nature of his job. His bank account, like weights, pulled him down into a sea of unease.

One evening, he ran into Eduardo on his way out of the office from the division adjacent to Melvin. Eduardo, the great-grandson of a Peruvian chief, had a jawline straight from the Andes and beard stubble rumored to inspire poetry. He was a fixture at SuperTech. Popular. Very knowledgeable.

Melvin found Eduardo at the end of the hallway, and even though it was the end of the workday, his linen blazer was wrinkle-free.

"Hi, Eduardo."

"Yo, Melvin, *cómo estás?*"

The two of them fist-bumped and headed to the parking lot, Eduardo's popularity inviting greetings and salutations as they walked.

"Qué pasó?"

"Eduardo!"

"Have a good weekend!"

Eduardo reciprocated with waves, nods, and shout-outs. When they got to the exit, Eduardo held the door open for Melvin as he lobbed comments and questions back to the security officers.

"Got a big weekend planned?"

"Holiday weekend, just hanging out with the family. Have a good one, Eduardo!"

"You too!"

Eduardo followed Melvin through the door, sighing.

"Oh, man, I forgot," he said. "Holiday weekend."

Melvin looked at him as they walked, waiting for him to continue.

"Family get-together, man," he unbuttoned his blazer and shook his head. "Siblings."

"Some tension there, I'm guessing?"

"*La tirantez,*" Eduardo said under his breath as he put both hands in his pockets and looked down at the sidewalk. Then, looking up, "Yeah, well, I don't know if I'd label it as tension." They turned the corner at the end of the sidewalk. "More like just a lot of competition ... which I guess is like tension." He tapped Melvin with the back of his hand and said, "Hey, how about *competension*?" He overenunciated the word to emphasize the change. "We just made up a new word, Melvin."

Melvin raised his head and eyebrows in mock appreciation. A few steps later, he asked, "How many siblings?"

"There's three of us. I'm the middle child." Eduardo shrugged. "I know, *cliché*, right? The middle guy always trying to figure out where he stands with the others." He squinted at the light reflecting off parked cars. "I've always competed with them. I guess it's served me well here." He nodded back toward the SuperTech building.

"The competition part?"

"Yeah, brings out the best in me."

"Eduardo, have you always …,"—Melvin paused and waited for someone to pull out of their parking space and drive away—"have you always been happy at SuperTech?"

"Happy," Eduardo repeated. "Happy. I don't know. What do you mean?"

Melvin watched a car or two drive by, then said, "Do you ever think about the implications of all that SuperTech does around the world?"

They reached Eduardo's car. He opened the door of his late-model SUV and threw his bag in the back. "What kind of implications?"

Melvin leaned up against the adjacent car and said, "Third-world country people. I've seen images of what we do with old product, where we dump it, *how* we dump it, what it's doing to the health of those who live there. It's not good."

Eduardo leaned against his car. He faced the setting sun and the SuperTech complex, looking at Melvin to his left and tapping the roof of his car with his right hand. "Melvin, are we doing anything illegal?"

"No," Melvin replied, then scratched his head and said, "Well, I don't think so. I mean, our legal guys are all over it. I think we have more lawyers working 'previously owned product placement' than in any part of the business."

Eduardo stopped tapping the car and looked at Melvin. "So, we're legal?" He summarized more than asked.

Melvin put his hands in his pockets, peered out over the parking lot, and said, "I guess." After a moment of silence, Melvin glanced at Eduardo and said, "It's not a good look for SuperTech, and it's definitely not good for the people on the receiving end. I think it might even be harmful, and if that's the case …" He let his sentence trail off as he glanced at Eduardo again.

"You know, Melvin, I'm not sure." Eduardo pushed the remote ignition. "Some people might be left behind. But if that's what the law allows for, then we just gotta trust the legal system will do the right thing in the end." He got into his seat as his driver window whirred open. He looked at Melvin, waiting for a response.

Melvin remained still against the other parked car, hands in pockets, looking down at his feet. He said, "Competension?" Then looked at Eduardo.

Eduardo furrowed his eyebrows for just a moment but then smiled, white teeth catching the sunset. "Yeah, I think so, Melvin. Ha, Competension!" He nodded and slowly accelerated out of his parking spot. "That's the word, Melvin. We just have to be content with that and be thankful we're on *this* end of things." He extended knuckles outside the window. Melvin reciprocated.

"Keep believing, Melvin." They bumped fists. "Don't lose the faith."

Melvin watched him pull out, exit the parking lot, and drive out of view. He sighed, found his car, and began the drive home, negotiating traffic while negotiating the pros and cons of talking to his wife. He never made up his mind. By the time he got home,

and Samuel jumped in his arms
and the three of them had dinner
and ran an errand
and returned home
and he lay down with Samuel for bedtime prayers
and buried his head under the pillows
the whole idea was buried.

And the following night as well.

· · · · ·

HOPE knew something was off. She wasn't a big believer in something so exclusive as women's intuition. She was more inclined to believe in a universal human intuition, but nevertheless, Hope, a woman, couldn't deny the uneasy feeling that her husband was treading challenging waters.

Things looked okay on the outside, but they didn't feel right on the inside. She probed the situation, floating little depth charges of questions out and around Melvin. She gained as much information as possible when he brought the body language home from work: protracted moments of silence, wandering sentences, foot-tapping. But she couldn't entirely break through to him.

So she decided to wait.

Initially, the waiting did nothing for her but stir up an old nail-biting habit. In between her pointer and middle fingers, she began to experiment with new approaches and new ways of thinking. She actively engaged in practices to free her mind. *Or was it to be mindful?* She couldn't remember; either way, she kept at it.

She googled *prayer* and YouTubed *grace*.
She podcasted *patience* and Instagrammed *trust*.
She dialed in her diet and discovered an allergy to goat cheese.
She dialed in her exercising and weirdly discovered an allergy to goat yoga.
Who knew?

She expanded her reading, things she considered "of depth." Which meant anything written by Dorothy Day, or the prophet Isaiah, or Howard Thurman, or the first four books of the New Testament, the ones not written by the Apostle Paul. Hope, for good or bad, didn't relate much to anything written by the Apostle Paul.

Reading.
Questioning.
Praying.
Why is Melvin acting so guarded?
Did he make a mistake?
Is this punishment?
Does love punish?

As she leaned into the questions, something like a melody emerged in and around her life, accompanied by a gentle but steady rhythm. In this way, she began to see waiting as something active and dynamic rather than passive and dull.

The rest took on as much importance as the notes.

The waiting became just as important as the action.

Hope became a more artful person for all these practices, but Melvin benefited as well. It was the space, the maturity, and the grace Hope afforded him that gave him the room to gain his bearings, to find himself, and to talk.

· · · · ·

ONE night as Melvin quietly closed the door to Samuel's

room, he began to open his heart. "Hope," he asked, standing still, both hands lingering on the doorknob behind him, "can we talk?"

Hope muted the TV, fluffed some pillows and sat up straighter. Melvin plopped onto the couch and laid his head back. He took a deep breath and said, "I've been putting this off for a long time. Look, I know our life has seemed better since I started working for SuperTech, but …,"—he exhaled—"it's a mirage. It's not better. It's worse. I've made a mistake, and I need to tell you."

Hope remained calm and receptive.

Then, in a rush of a sentence, he said, "SuperTech is involved in immoral business practices. There's a lot of innocent people getting hurt. I'm pretty sure I've got proof it's illegal. And I'm hopelessly mixed up in the middle of it all."

Hope was relieved it wasn't something with the marriage that had caused Melvin to distance himself. She waited for Melvin to say more.

Melvin, in the pause, glanced sideways at her. He dipped his head slightly, waited, then said, "Hope, I have a terrible employer. I don't know what to do. I'm in the middle of something bad!"

"Oh. Yes, I heard you. I was just processing." She reached her hand out to his. "I'm sorry."

"The worst thing is,"—Melvin squeezed her hand and

looked right at her—"I've known from pretty much the beginning, but I didn't tell you."

"Why didn't you tell me?"

Melvin sighed and laid his head back on the couch again. "I don't know. When I first considered it, I told myself I wanted to protect you. But the more I've thought about it, the more I've realized it has less to do with protecting you than it has with protecting my own insecurity about my misgivings with SuperTech, about how I made a mistake from the very beginning."

He shook his head, "I should've never started with them."

"But how would you have known?"

"That's the hard part. On my very first day, before I started anything, they had me sign a bunch of legal papers stating that I couldn't share any information with anyone about what they did." He turned again to look at her. "Hope, I signed something that said if I ever disclosed what they were up to, I would lose my job and be sued."

"Oh." Hope began to feel the gravity of the situation. It was her turn to sit back and exhale. "What ...,"—she started, then stopped, then started again—"What can you do? Is there anything you can do about it? Does management know?"

"That's the most ridiculous part. I'm confident everyone in management knows what's going on. I'm sure it's the reason they required me to sign my life away in the first place."

She sat up, turned her body toward her husband. "They don't own you, Melvin. You ... we'll do the right thing."

"Babe, we'll be doing the right thing without a job—and facing a lawsuit!"

She rubbed her forehead and sank down into the couch, softly pounding her head against the backrest, whispering to no one in particular, "Damn it. Damn it."

They sat in silence. Melvin began to say something, but the bedroom door opened and out stumbled Samuel. He dragged his blanket across the living room floor and crawled up and onto Hope's lap, laying his head down on her chest. He was back asleep in a matter of seconds. Hope held him close.

Melvin sat up, leaned over, and put his head in his hands. He said, down into the floor, "I'm just going to have to resign."

"Yeah ...," Hope said, mechanically stroking her son's hair. "I mean, what else can you do?"

A few wordless minutes later, Melvin stood up and walked by Hope, dragging his fingers lightly across her arm as he went by and to bed. He didn't bother to disrobe. He lay, stomach down, and went to sleep.

Hope rearranged Samuel and lay on the couch with him, her body attempting to stretch out all the implications.

She looked across the room sideways. Blinking slowly. She dozed in and out of sleep, in and out of dreams.

. . . . .

HOPE'S childhood room was a makeshift space: an old back porch reimagined into a bedroom. It was fashioned, not unlike the relationship that created Hope, without permit or license: a mutiny of a structure, stumbling out of the back corner of a home, out of the back corner of an uninspiring neighborhood.

Hope's perception of the room at eight, nine, or ten years of age was a bit different, of course. She'd had the growing awareness that it wasn't the choicest space, but it was all she had. It became something of a sanctuary for her, a respite from the chaos dominating the rest of the home. What the room lacked in design and planning, it made up for in other ways. She actually loved the windows that had replaced the screens, even if they were thin, unevenly hung, and always in need of cleaning.

She would close the door and the house behind, open the curtains and the world in front. She often envisioned herself on a great veranda, overlooking a terrace of gardens, lined with palm trees, royal, and date. It was her favorite place to read and write, to reflect and think.

Her room was where she read about the courage of

Frodo, the selflessness of Nyasha, the precociousness of Matilda, and the audacious dreams of Imani.

Her room was where she penned several short stories about a bunny named Hoper. She shared the stories with a few friends who read the bunny's name as Hopper. Hope was incredulous. No one saw *her* name tucked inside the bunny's name? No one recognized the obvious? *It's supposed to be pronounced with a long o!*

Her room was where she first read the Bible. It came to her by way of a young mother from the Greek Orthodox church down the street. The lady stopped in to see Hope's mother on occasion. One day she brought a meal and the book. Hope stood in the doorway and watched the visitor, mesmerized by her stately nose and the rope braids in her long black hair. Hope unconsciously touched her own nose, smiling when the lady waved.

Later that evening, Hope attempted her own rope braids. Then Bible in hand, she dramatically unfurled the curtains and sat down in her beanbag chair, imagining their beautiful Greek visitor, wherever she lived, sitting down to read the holy book in the very same fashion. Hope understood little of what she read—but the part about the Hebrew man teaching, and healing, *and then being killed?* That caught her attention. She thought long and hard about the crucifixion.

She spent a lot of time in her room, and eventually,

years later, it was where she heard from God. Or George Orwell.

It was Hope's second semester of her senior year of high school. She was slightly concerned about GPAs, scholarships, and colleges. She knew English lit offered her the quickest way to earn extra credit, which led her to Orwell's novel *1984*.

It was a quiet Saturday
afternoon.
Spring.
An eraser propped one of the windows open.
A breeze.

She sat in her beanbag chair. Clouds, like drapes, opened and closed. Alternating shafts of sunlight swept across the room, across her body, across her fingers picking at the floor's cracked and peeling paint.

She read about *1984's* protagonist, Winston. The pressure he felt, the fear of the totalitarian regime. Big Brother watching. His anxiety. The guilt over his subversive and unlawful thoughts. The impending doom. The panic when he noticed a woman watching and following.

Hope pulled her hair behind her ears, sat up, and held the book with both hands.

Continuing, she read about Winston in a crowded

marketplace. The interaction with the woman. The wordless exchange. The note inside Winston's pocket. His heart sinking. The fear. The realization he'd been found out. His searching for a safe space to read the note. Preparing for the worst. The reality. The judgment. And then the shock! The message was a complete reversal of what he had imagined. All the note said was,

I love you.

The further she read, the further she identified with the protagonist. She, at some subterranean level, recognized *his* uneasiness as *her* uneasiness.

Maybe it was her broken home, the cracks of which invited so much darkness. Maybe it was the absent father, the silence of whom caused so much noise. Maybe it was her season of life, the anxiety of leaving home, the struggle to consider herself worthy of moving on to college.

Whatever the case, Hope heard someone speaking to her in that makeshift room, that makeshift home, stumbling out of the back corner of that uninspiring neighborhood. It took her completely off guard. She wasn't looking for it. But she *heard* it. There wasn't a trace of guilt or embarrassment. Not a hint of scolding or shame. No demand for sacrifice or penance. None of that. All it said was,

I love you.

When she heard those words, it was as if the discordant soundtrack of her life, full of so much noise and suspension, suddenly resolved into a singular tone. It sparkled and grew into a chord that pulsed and swept through the room.

She closed the book
quietly.
Her eyes
slowly.
She sunk down into the sound as deeply as she could.
Beanbag crunching,
Forming, reforming around her body.

She hugged the book across her stomach. She felt the patterns of cloud and light across her face, a secret morse code of a message.

The smell of spring rain was in the air.

And she was loved.

. . . . .

HOPE opened her eyes early the following morning. She carefully moved Samuel's arms and legs. She sat up. She hadn't heard from God, but as the sun rose, she began to unearth a measure of conviction. It was just a seed, but the more she considered it, the more she felt it opening deep within her.

She walked into their bedroom. She shook Melvin's

shoulder with one hand and bit a fingernail on the other hand.

"Melvin." She put her hands on her hips and looked out the window, waiting a moment, then whispered intently, "Melvin! Wake up!"

He rubbed his eyes.

She started in, "You can't walk away from this."

He propped himself up on elbows. "What?"

She crouched slightly, almost fighter-like. "Melvin, you can't walk away from this."

"Walk away from what?" He asked, wiping his eyes in confusion, then falling back into his pillow as he remembered his dilemma, the choice he would have to make, the consequences.

"I've been thinking ..."—Hope started to pace back and forth—"look, you're a good man, with a good heart ..." She offered up fragments of sentences within the rhythm of her pacing. "If people are suffering ... if what you say is true, there are too many people getting hurt, and truthfully ...,"—she turned to pace back the way she came—"if only *one* person is being hurt, what are you going to do?"

With one hand raised and the other pressed against her forehead, she asked again, "What are you going to do—quit? And let that one person get hurt?" She dropped her hand as her voice dropped into a kind of guttural whisper.

"No, we're *not* backing down from these people. We're going to fight!"

Melvin wiped his eyes again, waited for her pacing to slow down, then countered her passion. "Wait, this is going to be very complex. Maybe I can fix it."

"I've been thinking about ways to fix this all night." Her voice softened a bit as she sat on the edge of the bed. "I'm not sure this is exactly fixable, Melvin. If you leave without saying anything, innocent people lose. If you fight, we lose your job. If you stay, we lose our self-respect. Nothing about this is simple."

"Babe, what about the future—"

"Screw the future, Melvin." She leaped to her feet and narrowed her eyes. "What are we? Hostages? No. We're not. They can't tell us how to live our lives. We'll allow them to make things right, but if they don't, we'll do the right thing."

She looked out the window. "And ... and we'll make our *own* future. Yes, without money or ... or without a house, or ... or without our children ever going to college." She let out an involuntarily little laugh that came out louder than she'd anticipated.

She spun back toward Melvin. "The future's got enough worry of its own. We've never gone hungry, *or* ... *or* not had a roof over our heads, *or* been cold." She overenunciated each *or* as if reminding herself of their agency. "No, we're living for the present. Here and now. And right now?"—she pointed toward the ground—"right *now?* We know the right thing to do."

A smile appeared at the corner of Melvin's tired eyes, then spread across his face.

"What?" she demanded, then smiled as she leaned over and punched him in the shoulder. He laughed, pulling her down on top of him. She let out a shriek. Melvin wrapped her up in his arms and said, "You want to fight, don't you?"

"Stop it," she laughed while jabbing at his ribs.

Samuel, awakened by the noise, came running in from the other room, yelling. He was unaware of what was taking place, but he was thrilled to launch himself from the top of the footboard into the middle of the fray.

The three of them rolled around on the bed wrestling each other, wrestling their fears.

· · · · ·

EMBOLDENED by Hope, Melvin decided to speak to his superiors the next day.

Maybe someone would listen.
Maybe others at SuperTech would share his concerns.
You never know.
And...

Melvin's superiors didn't listen. And no, there weren't others at SuperTech who shared his concerns.

What was shared was a red-faced *SuperTech this* and a *SuperTech that!*
And a
SuperTech is the greatest company in the world!
And an expletive-laden
Who do you think you are, Melvin?

Security arrived. Then company lawyers. Melvin was escorted out of the building while being walked through a long list of contractual breaches he'd be making if he went to the authorities. The last of the warnings were read to him through his closing car window as he backed out of his parking space.

Leaving the parking lot, he called the government agencies Hope had preprogrammed into his phone the night before, which set a whirlwind in motion.

It was for Melvin and Hope a motion-blurred season of phone calls, meetings, last-minute childcare, part-time jobs, shuffling car seats, late-night legal reading, and countless conversations with the State Labor Department, the Federal Trade Commission, the DOJ, the FBI, the UN, the NBA, the WWF? It went on and on. There were a lot of acronyms involved.

The reactions from Melvin's friends at SuperTech came in at first like a smattering of rain:

Where were you today?
Hey, what happened?
There are all kinds of rumors flying around!

Then the messages quickly turned into a downpour:

This isn't fair. I'm going to talk to someone right now.
And
You're one of the best employees SuperTech has!

Only to die back down to a drizzle:

We don't know all the facts, but it doesn't seem right.
And
We're with you, Melvin.

Then an isolated drop or two:

Your integrity won't be forgotten.
And
Hey, you're still coming to Antonio's party next weekend, right?

Finally:

Do you remember the password to get the alarm on floor five turned off? Karen accidentally put in the wrong code.

The bulk of their relational fallout came and went within a few weeks. Their economic fallout took a little longer but was equally intense. The choice to be forthright, deal with the conflict, and shed light on what SuperTech's practices were doing to people all around the world invited all kinds of pain and suffering.

"Isn't it crazy," Hope said one day, "how the decision to align ourselves with people we *don't* know has caused us to be out of alignment with so many people we *do* know?"

. . . . .

MELVIN and Hope attempted to deal with the stress, each in their own way. Melvin bought a stress ball. It helped. But only for two weeks. Then it ruptured.

That afternoon he stormed out the door to return the defective product. The Finer Image manager cleared his throat in derision to point out that the store had never experienced anyone returning a stress ball before. But midsentence, he noted the wrinkled shirt and undomesticated nature of Melvin's gaze. The manager changed his mind, replaced the broken stress ball, and carefully handed a second one over for good measure.

When Melvin triumphantly returned with not one but two brand new stress balls, Hope roared with laughter. Caught up in the genuineness of her response, he began laughing too. The entire scenario reduced both of them to tears as Samuel stood slowly behind a pile of toy blocks, raising eyebrows, watching his parents slap legs and attempt to breathe.

Meanwhile, Hope imbibed heavily, deep into her cuticles for a few days, but then she ratcheted up previous disciplines. She carved out time to read, to question, to get to the bottom of what she was feeling, to reflect, to pray.

What she found reappearing was the same basic sequence of questions she'd asked previously. Church or no church. Suffering still existed.

Why is this happening?
What does it mean that we're going through this?
What does it mean that good people suffer?
What did it mean that God's son suffered?

He was supposed to be a representative of God, as she understood it, yet the way he lived his life was conspicuously free of sacrifice and judgment. *What kind of God is that?*

And he was also a representative of humanity, as she

understood it. Yet he seemed to have no need to project anxiety and fears onto a deity, to get the deity to dislike the people *he* disliked. *What kind of human is that?*

It proved impossible for Hope to consider suffering and injustice without considering his journey.

What if he experienced pain despite being true and good?
Wait, what if he experienced pain precisely because he was true and good?
What if his distress was a window into the distress of God?

A God of distress?

She couldn't wrap her mind around what it meant, but like a song getting stuck in one's head, the idea wouldn't go away.

Melvin wrestling with Samuel: she heard the melody as a form of *gentleness.*

An acquaintance working through problems with their spouse: the melody as a type of *forgiveness.*

A documentary about a family disowning their son because he was gay: the melody as something *wounded.*

The song ebbed and flowed, in and out, foreground and background, but it never fully receded.

One morning she went on her daily run with Samuel.

She and the little guy had worked out an agreement. It was her job to run and push. It was Samuel's job to point out different trees: big ones, little ones, green ones, brown ones. He was very good at it, little finger sticking out of jogger-stroller like E.T.

Hope was smiling, thinking about the beauty of her son and the beauty of the trails that wound through the foothills where they ran, when she noticed an elderly couple off to her left. The couple was standing in front of a park bench. The wife carried an unfocused look. The man stood at her side, put his hand on the back of the park bench, and began leaning toward her.

Hope followed the path around the clearing, slowing her pace, watching in between trees to see what the man was doing.

His leaning.
Speed of a glacier.
Lips puckering.
The wife's countenance unaffected, like a lake at sunrise.

Hope slowed to a walk, then stopped, holding her breath, concerned the man might fall over. But finally, his lips touched his wife's cheek. The lady gave no response. Hope exhaled and quickly ducked her head. She began walking again. Then she pulled her hair behind her ears to steal another glance. She watched the man reposition himself upright, reach for his wife's hand, help her stand, then gently begin to lead her away.

Hope walked faster, then jogged, then ran, the emotion of the moment fueling a faster pace. Samuel squealed with delight, but Hope couldn't hear him. The melody was back, within her, all around her, and it sounded like *endurance* or *commitment* or *humility.*

They followed the melody throughout the park, all the way home. She didn't stop until they arrived back at their front porch. She got Samuel and the stroller in the front door.

headphones yanked off,
tossed on kitchen table,
unbuckling Samuel,
opening doors to the balcony,
drinking bottled water,
rubbing forehead,
pacing.

Returning inside, she began rummaging through the junk drawer for pen and paper. She yanked out seven batteries and a bag of paper clips. She threw them up on the counter. Samuel toddled around her legs, humming and playing with a toy car. Hope bent closer, peering into the drawer. She found an old remote that stared back at her for a moment. She tossed it in the trash, followed by a mangled package of Post-it notes, an empty prescription bottle, and three Goldfish crackers. Finally, she located a pen and notepad.

She stepped back out to the balcony and slapped the notebook down on the coffee table. She sat down and started scratching out thoughts and ideas. She chewed her lip, starting and stopping, crossing out and underlining, writing and rewriting until she heard the song forming as a question.

She composed the question, sat back, and read it. Then jerked forward, grabbed the pen, scribbled through the entire page, and recomposed. Eventually, she left all the scratches and scribbles behind, turned to a clean sheet, took a breath, and in one clean stretch, wrote:

Suppose God isn't a projection, someone like us, only bigger, stronger, more powerful: a benevolently biceped Super-superman? What if God is more like a melody, the beauty of which opens our hearts to the powerless?

She laid the pen down next to the notebook quietly. She reread it and nodded. Hope hadn't set out to pen such thoughts. She just followed the music that ebbed and flowed, formed and reformed in the midst of her reading, in the midst of her questions, in the midst of her prayers, in the midst

of the SuperTech drama,
of losing so many friends,
of her rejection by the church,
which was really her rejection of their rejection of her,

of being a mom and a wife,
of feeling God say, "I love you,"
or was it George Orwell?

of reading books "on the veranda" as a child,
of her absent parents,
of all the extra pressure.

She read and reread her questions as she listened to the melody swell and ring out around her house. She took a deep breath and drank another bottle of water, the song growing and sparkling with the prism of colors refracting through the water in the bottle, then slowly emptying, fading away.

· · · · ·

SUPERTECH, of course, had its own way of dealing with stress.

Filing of ridiculous lawsuits.

Procuring of fabricated testimonies.

Posting of disparaging social media.

Hope and Melvin found themselves being un-friended, un-followed, and un-liked at an alarming rate. They watched their social worth, like the last gasp of a whimpering balloon, dramatically shoot out into the night sky. They didn't know whether to laugh or cry.

They did both.

Still, the young couple refused to quit. Hope had so many questions. *Is it the principle of the matter? Can we really win? Are we fighting out of pride and ego?* She didn't know the answers. But they kept going.

And then SuperTech's would-be *coup de grâce*: an invitation for other tech companies to join them in the fight. BigTech, MegaTech, and HugeTech.

Erstwhile raging rivals.

Cutthroat competitors.

Opposing organizations.

They fired up their private jets and conference calls, their indignation and solidarity. Backroom meetings and under-the-table dealings. They found, in the punishment of Melvin and Hope, a bridge to cross their differences.

· · · · ·

MELVIN and Hope bore the pressure admirably, but it took more out of them than either had anticipated. They logged countless hours assisting the acronyms without ever receiving assurance that truth would, indeed, prevail.

One evening, deep into the struggle, Hope rocked Samuel in the living room. The little family was exhausted. Melvin was seated on the couch opposite Hope, leaning over a coffee table scattered with takeout boxes and leftovers. Hope raised an eyebrow as she watched him. He was attempting to clean up using only his chopsticks. She rolled her eyes, then laid her head back and rocked some more.

She could feel Samuel's body warm against her, his head growing sweaty up against her neck. She felt the wood of the floor through her socks. She pushed against the hardness, asking herself, or Melvin, "Why do you think God's son had to die?"

"Because the people killed him," Melvin said, without looking up, concentrating more on chopstick skills than answers.

Hope slowed the rocking. "What?"

Melvin dropped the last leftover noodle into a trash bag, raising his arms in victory over accomplishing his task without using fingers.

Hope continued, "What if that *was* the reason? The only reason?"

She repeated his answer: "Because the people killed him. Is it that simple?" She adjusted the bundle of heat on her lap and started rocking again, feeling the coolness of the air across her neck.

Melvin got up to take the bag to the trash can. "I don't know, Hope." His ability to converse gone for the night, he used the last of his energy to poke her in the shoulder with a chopstick as he passed, saying, "I don't have a better answer than, 'I don't know.'"

Hope rocked silently but couldn't get to a better answer either.

Eventually, she carried her boy into his room and gently laid him in his bed. She leaned over the little portable railing installed to keep him from rolling off. She kissed his flushed cheek.

Lying here, in this little bed.

Her fingers traced the railing, the edges of his bed. Then she stood up, walked to the doorway, and paused. She chewed her lip as her eyes scanned the entirety of the doorway frame.

In this little room.

She leaned against the frame, sensing the melody returning, ebbing and flowing around the little incarnation she and her partner participated in each morning, crossing the threshold of two worlds, laying aside their adult status, their power, their import to be with their son.

She took a glance at Samuel as she went through the doorway, whispering, "There's nothing that could stop us from being with you." She entered the hallway, leaving her arm stretched behind her, hand on the doorframe as long as possible, as if attempting to leave something of herself with her son.

· · · · ·

THE ordeal dragged on. Depositions. Examinations. Preliminary hearings. Attorneys, agents, officials. The acronyms and *their* agendas. SuperTech's defense and *their* agendas. Most days Hope and Melvin felt like mice in a room full of cats.

Finally, after months of work, the acronyms brought official charges against SuperTech, which triggered all kinds of countercharges. A ridiculous amount of stuff: criminal, civil, parking citations, homeowners association fines, library fines, anything and everything.

The trial began. The couple showed up every day, together, side by side, he sometimes on the witness stand, both of them at the plaintiff's bench. Jan supported Hope and Melvin's struggle by sitting behind them in the gallery, by taking care of Samuel when she could, by questioning, challenging, and struggling with the powers in her own world.

They endured scores of cover-ups, accusations, and counteraccusations. Hope and Melvin experienced waves of anticipation and anxiety. The lawyers continually pulled them aside to coach, support, and direct. It was a grueling journey that left them most days with less confidence than they had the day before.

Meanwhile, SuperTech seemed to be in their element. They grew more and more energized throughout the process. They leveraged deep resources, retained the best lawyers, and identified the most pertinent loopholes. They fought, scrambled, choked, rolled eyes, pointed fingers, and hissed all the way to the end.

And then, after all the evidence, and prosecution, and examinations, and rebuttals, and closing arguments, the trial wound down. The judge thanked the jury and invited them to leave, deliberate, and decide. The court was adjourned. SuperTech's counsel filed out. Row after starched row.

Melvin and Hope received a few uncertain handshakes and less than positive glances from their legal team before heading to their car. It was a wet evening. They dodged their way across the street, doubt like raindrops peppering the papers they held above their heads.

They headed for home, tired. Quiet. There was little sound except for a few passing cars and the occasional swipe of the windshield wipers. Finally, Melvin, in an attempt to be positive, said, "You know, whatever happens, we've highlighted how broken the system is."

Hope's head leaned up against the passenger-side window. She was watching droplets of water skim and glance off the window, the remaining moisture being forced by the wind to flow, morph, and reform into a single stream from the front to the back of the window. Staring at the little stream, she said, "Actually, you could say the system's not broken at all."

Melvin furrowed his eyebrows and tapped the wipers.

Hope continued, "They're responding exactly as any well-oiled organization would respond. We keep telling people SuperTech is broken, that the whole industry is broken, but Melvin, it's not broken. In reality, it's working just like it's supposed to."

She adjusted her seat belt and sat up. "This is the design: if you believe in SuperTech, and you follow the rules of SuperTech, then you benefit ...,"—she overenunciated the S each time she said the company's name—"but if you *don't* believe, and you *don't* follow all the rules, you don't benefit. You're either in or out. That's what the system does, Melvin. No, the tech industry is working very well."

He veered the car around a few puddles.

"You know the worst part?" she continued. "The worst part is, in a way, we're culpable. I mean, in a bigger way, we're *all* culpable. We live in a society that creates these companies like SuperTech. When they make money, it fuels our economy. We benefit. We don't really care how they do it. We're just glad money's circulated. It brings us security. And if a little security is good, then a lot of security is even better, so let's …"—her voice crescendoed—"let's create more companies to do the same thing!"

She clinched and unclenched her fists. "We've done a terrible job, all of us, of asking questions, of holding people accountable, but, honestly, I have to look in the mirror. I've done a terrible job. What's wrong with me? I've helped create a society where systems are allowed to exist that benefit some and hurt others. Why? So I can have a better future? So my children and I can have *security*? Doesn't our country uphold the ideal of taking care of everyone? Of recognizing we all have unalienable rights? There are laws in place to keep us from harming people."

She bit back an acerbic laugh, thinking of all they'd learned about the law in recent months. "These are living, breathing humans! We keep uncovering all these statutes that are supposed to keep us from hurting people, but it doesn't seem to matter."

Melvin exited off the highway and into their community. "Yeah," he said, "the more laws we found that said, 'one can't take advantage of people,' the more loopholes we found that wind up allowing for companies like SuperTech to take advantage of people." Then, under his breath, he said,

"Because, you know, when you take advantage of people, *you really just wanna make sure you do it lawfully.*"

His sarcasm invited more silence.

But then Hope dropped her hands and sat up straighter. Melvin's quip opened her up to a new line of thinking. "It's like God's son," she said, at first half-whispering, then as she continued rising, repeating a bit louder, "it's like God's son. The story says the religious leaders killed God's son before sundown." Then, "Oh my God, Melvin. They rushed to have him killed before sundown so they wouldn't have to work on their holy day!"

She paused a moment waiting for Melvin to see what she was saying. She adapted his earlier line and said slowly, "Because, you know when you murder God's son ..."

Melvin finished the sentence: "*you really wanna make sure you do it lawfully.*"

The weirdness of the thought left them quiet for a minute as Melvin took a turn into their neighborhood. The rain slowed. It was quiet except for tires rotating over the wet pavement. Then Melvin asked, "But why? Why did he have to die? You've been asking that for months."

She shook her head and laid her head back against the headrest. "I don't think he had to die." Then she smiled, "But he did have to show up." She nodded and continued, "Love. It was love, Melvin. He loved us. There's nothing he wouldn't do to be with us. If you knew you might get killed, would you still take a chance to be with Samuel?"

Melvin pulled the car into their driveway and parked. "Of course. I wouldn't be able to *stop* myself from being with him."

"I know." She laughed. "It's like God's just unable to help himself. He *had* to be with us."

They smiled, their previous agitation dissipating in the presence of the outrageous news.

"Wait," Melvin lanced the moment. "How does that help us with the trial?"

Hope exhaled. "Well …" She hung on the word for a moment, drawing it out, then said quickly, "It probably doesn't."

"But—"

"Look, it's about love. I think you did this … we did this … out of love. I mean, it was just the right thing to do. We couldn't turn our backs on the people. We crossed the threshold. We followed the melody, like a trail, like an invitation, and entered into their world. Whether we win or lose, the beauty of it all has opened us up to others."

She undid her seatbelt and pivoted in her seat to face Melvin. There was a tear in the corner of one eye. Her voice grew quiet with conviction. "It's the way … to be in solidarity with people who are being taken advantage of … to be overwhelmed by the powers. Whether it was then or now, this is it. We might not win this case. We might lose everything, but this is still right, Melvin. We've already won. This is the way."

. . . . .

THE sun rose the following morning, burnt orange-yellow and expanding. It angled and filtered through window blinds to find the couple lying side by side. Hope blinked in the new day. Her mind rewound, slowly at first, then rapidly backward through the lengthy court proceedings and the pretrial's adrenaline. Then further, to the joy of their son's birth, the beauty of their wedding, and then further, to the day she'd met Melvin.

Chemistry class.
Paired up for homework.
Seated together.
Back corner of the room.

A cloud had passed, allowing a gleam of sunlight for a split second, first in the bracelet she was wearing, then as he turned toward her, in his eyes. The reflection went from burnt henna to almond. They held eye contact longer than one usually does at a first meeting. She heard her heart beating. Then she dropped her head, self-consciously. She knew he was still looking at her.

Hope was thinking through all these things when she realized Melvin was awake right at that moment, cheek to one side, looking at her. She glanced at him and smiled. He put his arm across her waist and said, "Life's been hard on Hope."

She pinched his arm. Melvin's phone buzzed at the same time as her pinch. He jumped, rubbed his eyes, looked at the phone, and said, "They've reached a verdict. It's time."

And so it was that they gathered later that morning, hearts in throats, with dozens of others around the courtroom awaiting the decision.

Jury filing in.
Everyone rising.
Judge entering.
Receiving paper from foreman.
Reading to himself.

Hope prayed for both her and Melvin, for Samuel, for their future. And then she landed on the faces of the innocent people who had been taken advantage of by SuperTech. She held them there in her mind's eye, wordlessly asking for help. Then Jan's face appeared in the mix, as well as people from church. She didn't deny the progression of faces, thoughts, movement, implications. She imagined herself standing with them. All of them.

They held hands and listened. A melody began playing over them, around them, from within them, ending with a beautiful suspended whole note,

    a fermata of
    risk and promise,
    chaos and hope.

And the judge read the verdict to all those who were listening.

The Cosmic Hum

For Shay and Caroline

In the beginning, there was music. Specifically, a musical chord: a trinity of notes consisting of a fundamental note, a third, and a fifth. We call these notes affection, grace, and friendship.

Sing with me, *hum, hum, hum.* No, really, hum some notes. There you go, yes, nice.

It was something of a Cosmic Hum.

So, in the beginning, there was a Cosmic Hum. Affection, grace, and friendship rang out and danced in ways that cascaded out into more notes: fourths, sevenths, and ninths, and dare I say elevenths? On and on, cascading out farther into even fainter notes that we sometimes call enharmonic overtones.

Enharmonic overtones are quieter background tones activated by more prominent sounds. If, for example, you pluck a guitar string then hold the body of the guitar up to your ear, you'll hear enharmonic overtones oscillating, weaving in and out of each other to the furthest corners of the audio spectrum.

And if there were a way to pick up the cosmos and hold it to your ear, maybe you'd hear all the enharmonic overtones responding to that original Holy Trinity of Notes oscillating, weaving in and out of each other.

Then again, maybe we're already picking up the cosmos and holding it to our ear because when the telescope at the Arecibo Observatory in Puerto Rico is pointed at space—specifically the space between planets and stars—it picks up a faint hum. It's the residual noise of the explosion from the creation of the universe 13.8 billion years ago, rolling out to the furthest corners of the cosmos. Astronomers call it electromagnetic radiation.

Yes, like I said, enharmonic overtones.

The Cosmic Hum. It's how everything began, the Holy Trinity of Notes and all the corresponding notes, sounds, and energy. It created the mountains and oceans and animals and gravity and calculus and sex and coffee and art and gluten-free cupcakes and laughter and joy and friendships. Everything was created by the excavating, energizing, related tones and overtones of Affection, Grace, and Friendship.

A particular song began to emerge in the Cosmic Hum's

relative minor key in the middle of all this procreation. Now, for the uninitiated let me explain a bit. A relative minor is quite similar to its major key. A minor, for instance, is the relative minor of the key of C major.

A minor is a scale existing within the larger context of the scale of C major.

A minor shares all the same notes as C major.

A minor and C major are forever intimately connected.

So, a song began to emerge in the relative minor key of the Cosmic Hum. It was a song called humanity. Humanity exists within a broader context of the Cosmic Hum. They share the same notes. They are forever intimately connected.

I don't have time to tell you about all of the stunning chords, vibrations, and notes that rang out of the song of humanity. Still, there's something we should talk about, something pertinent to our wedding celebration this evening, for, at a certain point, the song evolved in such a way that relationships formed, and people began to be intimately connected. That's right, the Holy Trinity of Notes created lovers, two people intentionally blending their music, and lovers sang the song of mothers and fathers. Before you knew it, a beautiful little melody was birthed called *children*.

In the same way that the key of humanity is related to the key of the Holy Trinity, so children are created in the relative minor key of their parents. That is to say, though children compose in different notes, they share the same scale as their parents. They are forever intimately connected.

For example, when a child is five years old, and the parent has to leave to go to work or out of town for a few days, the parent can tell the child, "No matter where I go, I will always hear your music. You're composing in a key that I know really, really well. Sing your song, and no matter where I'm at in the world or what's beyond this world, I will hear it."

Oh, and when the child is twenty years old and has to leave the parent, the child can say, "Mom, Dad, no matter where I go, I'll always hear your music. I know your key really, really well. Sing your song, and no matter where I'm at in the world or what's beyond this world, I will hear it."

And none of this is surprising because it's the same relationship that the parents have with the Cosmic Hum. For example, if you feel like the Hum has been absent, sing your song, and no matter what, the Hum will hear it. The Hum will always be with you. It doesn't fix everything, but it's with you, and it turns out we really don't need fixing; what we really need is someone to be with us.

And I'd like to say if the Hum is with us, *who can be against us?*

So, yes, the music rang out, and parenting was created.

And their music rang out, and children were created. And the children compose and sing and play, and with all their energizing vibrations, they grow and evolve. You just can't believe how much fun it is as a parent to hear your children's music, like, how they're in a relative key but also creating such interesting and unique melodies.

And then when the music of your child begins intersecting with the music of another child? When a boy and a girl meet? Oh, wow, it's super interesting. When young people meet, parents always step back and listen. Sometimes the music is out of tune and not very interesting, which causes the parent to grimace and wait patiently (or not so patiently) for the song to conclude. And then sometimes, as in the case of our children tonight, sometimes it's fascinating. And moving. And beautiful.

Yes, let's talk about our children tonight. From the beginning of their relationship, from the downbeat of their first date together, the music seemed very authentic. It wasn't exactly a date, except that as the evening concluded, when the boy had collected enough nonverbal cues to assure him that it was going well, he said, "Can we retroactively call this a date?"

And she smiled a beautiful smile and simply said yes.

So, yes, the opening notes were authentic and strong. It caught their attention. So much so that they decided by the second date—the very next night—to "take it slow."

And then they "took it slow" by being together for their first sixteen nights in a row.

The parents laughed and said, "What would this music sound like if they were taking it fast?"

Well, it's been a couple of years, and I'd like to say I'm glad things turned out the way they did because the music all of us hear is beautiful.

OK, something should be said about young people composing the music of marriage together: namely, that there are no shortcuts and no guarantees. It's not easy creating good music. Human beings, within the relative keys of the families they come from, are super complex. Blending individual sounds to make marriage sounds is dramatic and complicated. Throw in outside pressures. And inside anxieties. And randomness—sometimes out of tune in a benign sort of way, sometimes out of tune in a malevolent sort of way—and you will have all kinds of different notes, scales, and tunings. Honestly, the challenges are massive.

Good music is not created overnight. No matter what anyone says. Good music takes time. A couple has to practice. And learn scales. And theory. And study other great marriage music. But if they compose in the key of the Cosmic Hum, eventually art will emerge. It's the only thing a parent can promise a child. They cannot promise it will be easy. They cannot promise it will always be fun.

They can only promise that composing with Affection, Grace, and Friendship will eventually produce beautiful art.

(And while there's absolutely no pressure, and the couple should take their time composing, one day they will create in their relative minor and have children of their own. *And won't that be a fun song to hear?)*

Wrapping up now, what are the goals of all this music?

Well, it's not to make money. Boring. Been done a thousand times before. It's not global domination. That's a bad song. And the goal certainly isn't to allow awkward and discordant notes within the young people to surface and take control, though they will surface for sure. And for sure, the young couple will have to learn to exercise a measure of control. But, no, none of those are the goals. There is really only one goal …

Enjoy the music.

And remember to enjoy it within the context of the music that's ringing out over the cosmos all around. The young people have been created in the key of humanity, relative to the Cosmic Hum. And if they enjoy it, others will come along after them and say, "Oh, I'd like to create songs that way too! What key did you compose in?"

And then they'll laugh and say, "The key of the Cosmic Hum!"

Sing it with me now, c'mon, *hum, hum, hum.* And hold the notes out. Yes!

Play it. Sing it. Crank it up. The Cosmic Hum is with us every step of the way!

May you always hear the music.

May others, when they listen to your marriage, hear the music.

And may all of us in this world, and what's beyond this world, enjoy the music forever.

The Things Love Gives You

For Vinny and Courtney

One young day a man and woman met.

She was standing outside his front door. Not directly in front. Off to the side, leaning against the house, knocking, turning her head to look at the street. Peering out from underneath the porch at the depth of sky and the blue beyond. And he, on the inside. Stirring his arm that stirred a ladle that stirred a bubbling blend of tomatoey flavors.

Upon hearing the knock, he made his way to the front of the house, wiping his hands on a red-sauce-stained towel, glancing back at the kitchen, mind caught up in the culinary as it was.

With latch clicking and handle turning, she pivoted to face the opening, glancing back at the horizon, mind caught up in the clouds as it was.

Whoosh

And there, mid-whoosh, *he* came into view;
She forgot colors behind her, the intensity.
And there, mid-whoosh, *she* came into view;
He forgot flavors behind him, the tortellini.

Pulmonary systems lurched and stalled, but thankfully, a few stammering words served to jumpstart the moment. He leaned into the screen door that separated the two of them. She responded and stepped in closer. They spoke at length, he on one side of the screen door and she on the other.

Sun setting.
Skin tingling.
Sauce burning.

He asked if he could visit her sometime. She smiled and nodded her head.

So it was that a few days later, it was he on *her* front porch reaching for the doorbell, pausing to straighten out his shirt, then pushing the button. And before the dong could even follow the ding, the entrance flung open. They picked up where they had left off, each leaning in to the thin layer of metal mesh.

At the end of the evening, he took a deep breath. And a chance. He slowly stretched his hand out on his side of the screen: an invitation.

She smiled, ducked her head, pulled a strand of hair behind her ear. Then she mirrored the movement, the warmth slowly heating the cold screen between their two hands.

The very next night, they met again. He cooked dinner. She skipped up his steps and prepared to knock, but before her knuckles could land, he snatched the door open. They laughed and immediately pressed against the screen,

two
forehead-pocked
crosshatched
lovers.

After a few minutes, he walked backward down the hallway into the kitchen with his finger held up. She stood on her tiptoes, searching for a glimpse of the meal.

She smelled the sauces, the flavors.
Then he emerged with lasagna.
Yes, vegtable, her favorite!

And then they ate. He, of course, had to feed her through

the screen door. Which was difficult initially, but if he forcefully smashed the lasagna in and through the network of wires, eventually it reached her mouth. She loved it. She was so pleased to find he was a fantastic cook in addition to all of his other qualities.

They smeared lasagna and laughed, and talked, and ate for a long time. Then he smashed and splashed *crème brulee* and coffee to her. Later, he threw several glasses of water through the screen before finally pulling the hose from the kitchen sink down the hallway, then spraying everything down. Sauce. Icing. Coffee. Love.

The relationship continued. Week after week. Month after month. Her front porch. His front porch. They squished, squashed, and splashed food to each other. Sometimes dinner was followed by a movie. Gazing through the mesh didn't yield the best viewing experience, but they were happy to be at the front door together.

They leaned together so often that each of their screen doors began to rip. His enough that she could shove her hand through to his side. And hers enough that he could fit his arm through to her side. It was inevitable that arms would get scratched, poked, and punctured with such activity, but losing small pieces of flesh was a small price to pay for love. The young couple bandaged themselves up and did it all over again the very next night.

The relationship went on for five years. And then one

day, while on her front porch, he got down on one knee. She could barely see, so she pressed her face up against her side of the screen and poked an eye out through a hole.

Ah, so romantic.
He down on one knee.
She with her eye
sticking out of the screen.

He said, "I have an important question to ask."
She held her breath and said, "Yes?"
She began to tear up—yes, because of emotions, but also because her eye was getting scratched by tiny, jagged wires.
He continued, faster and louder than he had rehearsed, "I'd like to invite you over and open this screen door. Would you please consider coming into my house?"
She leaped into the air and screamed, "Yes!"
Unfortunately, when she jumped, she scraped her eye and later had to have surgery, but it was worth it because she was in love. And he was thrilled because he was in love. They pressed against the screen and did their best to embrace each other.
And then the big day arrived. She brought her family over to his house. She knocked on the door as she had the first time they met. He opened the front door and, *this* time, the screen door as well.

The family gathered around the young couple. The minister said a few things. "Is there anyone opposed to this door being opened?" And "This door opening is a holy moment." And "You know the door doesn't just let the bride in or the groom in, it lets the whole family in. No, seriously, do you promise to keep the door open until you die?"

And they both said, "Yes, yes, a thousand times, yes!"

And the minister continued, "What you are doing is difficult. And complex. And not done without risk. Sooner or later, you'll be let down, misled, wounded. Your heart will be broken. You'll hurt more than you can imagine because you will have opened the screen door wide and, in doing so, will have allowed the other so far into your life that you won't be able to separate where you end and where they begin. This will transform you in deep, profound ways. None of us really sign up for transformation. We're more interested in salvation."

The minister said other things that were deep and profound, but most people were there for the drinks, so he quickly wrapped it up and said, "And so on and so forth, by the power vested in me, the door is officially opened!"

Everyone cheered, the music played, and the young lovers embraced. Then they held hands and backed up a step or two. They took a good long look, for neither of them had previously viewed the other without looking through a screen door.

He thought: *This is good. Yes, very good.* Although there were a couple of minor surprises. He looked at her again. *Hmm, interesting: she has three eyes.* But it didn't matter. He shook his head. Honestly, he loved her eyes, even the extra one, and so he said to himself: *This is great, one more eye to get lost in when I'm staring at her.*

She spun around, gazed back, and nodded affirmatively; *yes,* she thought, *this is nice.* But she picked up on some things as well. For example, she noticed he had a lot of hair. A *lot* of hair. She craned her neck to see it running up and down his arms and neck. She was very much in love with him, but she had to admit it was startling to see so much hair. Without the screen door blocking the view, she realized he was really more wolf-like than human-like. It was kind of an odd look. But she said to herself and others, who asked later, "Honestly, I love dogs, and wolves are just like dogs. So, this is great. Yeah, this is ... this is great."

And so they celebrated.

Later, after everyone gave hugs, left, and went home, the two of them were alone. They sat down on the couch. He put his arm around her. She had to move some hair to find a comfortable spot, but then she leaned up against his shoulder.

Her eyes darted around the room as she rewound their courtship. *How did I miss all the hair?*

His hand patted her shoulder. *Three eyes? I get it now. She's always noticing things before me.*

Suddenly, she sat up and looked at him. And he sat up and looked at her. She said, "You know? I thought you were giving me everything I ever wanted. And you are." She stood up and took a couple of steps, then spun to face him. She sighed, "But you're also giving me some things I don't want." Then she locked eyes on him—all three of them—smiled, and said, "But, you know what? I want you, so I receive it. I take all of you."

Then, as if they had decided beforehand how the staging should go, he stood up, and she sat down. He traced her steps, spun, and said, "Wow, I thought I knew love before we opened the screen door." He scratched his head in thought, though he really had to dig to get under all the hair. "Yeah," he laughed, "I admit, this is more than I imagined." He looked at her and said, "But I take you. All of you. I love you."

And they embraced
the things they wanted
and the things they didn't.

Hovering

Joseph gripped the rope tightly as he led the donkey down a rocky ravine. He felt the fibers digging into his hands, the heat from the friction. He glanced up at his young wife shifting and swaying with the animal. She was looking down, carefully watching hooves navigate dusty stone and gravel.

The three of them—Joseph, Mary, and donkey—descended without speaking, the only noise the shuffling of rock, the scraping of hoof, the occasional grunt of Joseph guiding and pulling the animal. Mary dipped and swayed with one last kick of the donkey's legs up and over the edge. The mountains rippled off to the north as if a giant muscular arm had swept the land in front of them, leaving it smooth and endless. The trail snaked down a gentle slope for a bit, then, under the rush of clouds, made a straight run out to the edge of all they could see.

Mary began speaking again, picking up where she had left off, talking about empires and emperors.

"What's old Octavian calling himself again?" Mary asked. She squinted off into the horizon, shaking her head, thinking about the pain of being forced to take another census.

"I think he's going by Caesar Augustus now," Joseph replied.

"Caesar Augustus? Like his uncle Julius? Do you imagine every dictator coming out of Rome now will call themselves Caesar?"

Joseph laughed. "Probably."

Mary shook her head. "I don't like it," she said.

"His name change, or what he's forcing us to do?"

"I don't like either one," she quickly answered. "Although I don't blame him. Octavian is an unfortunate and moronic name. If that were my name, I'd change it too. Sounds like something you'd name, oh, I don't know, a donkey or something." She patted the donkey's neck and said, "In fact, that's what I'm going to start calling our donkey here. Octavian, the ass."

Joseph laughed again. "I like it," he said, "but if we cross paths with the authorities in Bethlehem, maybe it would be best to not mention's the donkey's name."

"Yes," Mary raised her voice, "onward Octavian the ass. Drag the poor and the tired, the weak and the pregnant across the desert to Bethlehem." A raven landed close by, but Mary didn't notice; she was busy thrusting her fist to the sky. "Yes, oh mighty ass, you must count us and get our tax money, to figure out your labor force, to build your worthless armies." The raven ducked its head and immediately flew away.

Joseph watched the bird and thought, *I don't blame you, bird*. He draped the rope over the neck of the donkey, confident he didn't need to guide the animal as much while on level ground. He patted the animal's neck, feeling the coarse hair between his fingers. "Good ol' Octavian," he said.

A few minutes later, Joseph heard a small but distinct *ping*. He turned to locate the sound and immediately squinted as light reflected off a small piece of metal in the air. He realized Mary had pulled a drachma out of the leather pouch tied around the donkey's neck. She was flipping the coin in the air.

"Hey." Joseph laughed. "Be careful with that." She caught it, scrunched her nose, and looked at the image of Caesar Augustus.

She handed it to Joseph and asked, "What's it say again?"

He wiped the coin with the sleeve of his tunic, then read the inscription. He rolled his eyes and said, "Prince of Peace and Lord of Lords."

It was her turn to roll her eyes. "Prince of Peace," she

mumbled, "imagine calling yourself Prince of Peace after you slaughtered half the known world, including our little Jewish world? My uncle and your father ..." Her voice trailed off.

Joseph grimaced at the thought of the men she mentioned, of the arrogance of Rome, of being forced to live in occupied territory.

"You think any of these Caesars will ever learn, Joseph? Hebrew lives matter!"

Joseph sighed. He squinted out to the deepest, thinnest line of blue on the horizon. *When would God help?*

He reached his arm up, found the pouch, and carefully reinserted the coin. He felt around at the bottom of the bag to confirm the money was safe. He kept his hand close to Mary as he looked up at her.

Mary was unlike anyone he had ever known. There were obvious things: the beauty of her face, the humor in her personality. Features of which he was certain. And then there were the less obvious things, things he couldn't quite name: the way she carried herself even on backs of donkeys, and her eyes, fiery and cobalt, the depths of which seemed to throb against the blue of the desert sky behind her as she returned his gaze.

Looking up at her, squinting through one eye, attempting to take her in, he said, "You're like royalty, Mary."

It was her turn to laugh. "What?" she asked.

Joseph nodded his head, then looked forward, patting the donkey's neck as he walked. "I was around Herod's family once, you know, Herod the Great."

"Herod the Great," she scoffed. "Should be Herod, the Terrorist."

Joseph smiled and raised his arms. "I know, I know, let me finish. A few years ago, I was in Jerusalem when his entourage came through. People, chariots, money, and the way the ladies, well, the way *all* of them carried themselves. They acted like they were worth something, but it was just a show." Joseph, still looking and walking forward, pointed up at Mary, "But you, you *know* you're worth something."

The smallest of smiles appeared at the corners of Mary's pursed lips as she looked at the top of Joseph's head. She squeezed the finger he still had stretched toward her. She took a deep breath and looked out over the desert.

"I don't know if I'm royalty, but I *am* blessed. What God is doing for us will never be forgotten. His mercy flows, like those sand dunes over there, in wave after wave on those who are in awe before him. He shows his strength and scatters the bluffing Octavians of this world. Just wait, Joseph, you'll see."

This was not the first time Joseph had heard Mary talk like this. But, *unlike* the first time, he was now considering believing her. Maybe God really was doing something inside of her. *Maybe she really is royalty.*

The conversation, like the landscape around them, grew sparse. Mary pulled her shawl over her head to keep her black hair from absorbing all the afternoon heat. For a long time, the only sound was Octavian's occasional snort or tail swish.

That evening they sat by the fire as it popped and cracked. The smoke was tentative, curling in and around sticks and logs, gaining courage, winding upward. Mary followed the smoke trail until it became lost within a sheet of sequin stars, itself lost within an ocean of black.

Joseph poked at the fire with a stick. Then he leaned back against the donkey and said, "Mary, tell me again what the angel said to you."

He watched her looking up into the sky. Her countenance reflected shades of oranges and yellows, heat and light. She looked at Joseph for a moment, then back up as if seeing the angel above her that very moment. She repeated what the messenger had spoken in short soft sentences, "A Holy Spirit will come upon you. The power of the Most High will *overshadow* you. Your offspring will be called holy. A son of God."

Joseph tried to find a Holy Spirit in the night sky as he thought about God's presence hovering over Mary. "Hey," he said, "do you remember what Torah says about creation?"

"Which part?" She moved her leg as a log cracked open by her foot.

"Right at the beginning." He leaned over to flick a fiery ember back into the fire. "In the beginning, God created the heavens and the earth. The earth was formless and void. Darkness was over the surface of the deep, and the Spirit of God *hovered* over the waters."

Joseph felt a rise in Mary's energy. It was more than just the reflection of fire or stars. There was something alive in her eyes. She smiled and nodded. She stared up at the stars again and said, "Yes … the Spirt of God hovered …"

Joseph sat up straighter. "Do you think …," he began to ask, then quieted as he began to be overwhelmed by the thought.

"Yes, I *do* think. I think the Spirit of God hovered over the waters of the deep, creating something out of the chaos of all that was. It's more than, well,"—she looked into the flames lapping up and into the air—"it's more than that he created out of nothing. He hovered over what was *already* there. It was the *wildness* of the face of the deep; he ordered it, he energized it."

"Without God, it would have just been chaos," Joseph chimed in.

"Yes, lost and without form. But God made something new. He took what was there and made something *new*." She placed both hands over her enlarged belly and finished the thought. "Joseph, I think he's doing something new again."

And for the first time since Mary's outlandish announcement, Joseph thought about hope. He felt warmth. It wasn't the fire. *This* warmth was spreading from the inside out. But then he hesitated for a moment, which kept the heat at bay. He held it there as he recalled what she had been like when she had first told him the news of her pregnancy: on her knees, fists coiled, pounding the tops of her legs, tears running down her cheeks, begging Joseph to believe that she really *had* been visited by an angel.

He remembered the bitterness.
Her tears.
His anger.

He toyed with returning to that emotion, that feeling that had defined him most of the previous year. He thought about reengaging anger, something to corral and control the vulnerability he felt. But the moment he began to push hope down and return to the pain, his thinking changed.

Why?
Why would I return to that?
Why would I choose to be bitter?
Why do I imagine that life is better if I'm in control?
What does it even mean to be in control?
No, that's not who I'm going to be.

Mary's words, like the smoke curling and dancing around the fire, were curling and dancing around Joseph. *Joseph, I think he's doing something new again.*

He lingered in the threshold of hope and control. And then chose hope. The sense of warmth welled up within, then seemed to lift out and into the heavens.

Mary shifted up on her knees and faced him. He turned his body to look squarely into her face. He whispered, "God's hovering over us as he hovered over the foundation of the world, isn't he?"

Her cheekbones lifted, her eyes an opening aperture, a witness to the energy he felt. She slowly nodded. "Yes," she said quietly. Reverently. Her countenance *so* strong, her spirit *so* fierce.

And the sky flashed with the testimony of a shooting star.

And embers, like tiny emissaries, drifted away with invitations.

And the creosote wood burned the fragrance of something new.

It was *so* real that Joseph actually looked up above him to see if the Spirit of God was hovering over them at that very moment. Mary snatched a tear from her eye and laughed watching him peer into the heavens. They both lay back against Octavian, the donkey. Mary eventually dozed off inside the crook of Joseph's arms, but Joseph didn't sleep well that evening. He feared the extraordinary and holy moment would eventually dissipate just as the fire at their feet was dissipating. So, throughout the night, he woke himself to search for the Spirit of God hovering. Above them. All around them.

Author's Note

We don't know the end of our story any more than Joseph and Mary knew the end of their story. Life is risk. Risk cannot be corralled, coerced, or controlled. The only thing we can expect is the unexpected.

But if God hovered over and lived within the chaos 13.8 billion years ago and made something new …

And if he hovered over and lived within the chaos of Mary's life and made something new …

He can hover over and live within the uncertainty of politics, the wildness of ecological crisis, the insecurity of racism, the unpredictability of pandemics, and he can hover over and within you.

You are being invited.
Right now.
In this moment.
In this moment.
And now, in *this* moment.
To risk. To hope. To love.

It's an invitation that's been going on for all eternity. It's our origin and our end, though using the word *end* within the context of an ever-changing, dynamic Spirit of love seems to be pointless.

All endings are really beginnings.

When the sermon this Sunday deals with eschatology—you know, the "end times"—just remember that the Greek word *eschWaton* is translated not only as "end" but also "edge." Don't find the preacher in the lobby afterward and make a big deal out of all of it. Just find them and give them a hug. Hold them long enough that it starts to feel weird. Pray over them, with them, around them.

Breathe.
Be patient.
Be entangled.

Wait about a year. No, three. Then tell them about *the edge*.

The Spirit hovers along the edge of all we are. If you listen, out in the desert under a panoply of stars, or in the stillness of your own heart, you can hear the movement of air, the deepest *whoosh* of wings oscillating over all the uncertainty. You're being invited to live at the edge, to let go of fear, to stop trying to control. You're being invited into liberation from anxiety.

If we recognize the Spirit is hovering over us, willing to partner with us in the very contractions of our chaos, something miraculous and new could be birthed in our world. And our world desperately needs it.

Don't give up.

About the Author

Jonathan is an award-winning and best-selling amazon author of four books. The faith community evolving at missiofaith.life is where he spends a lot of his time, and he's incredibly proud of what's happening at LQVE.org. When he's not with his family, he's studying open and relational theology. Or hiking. Or both.

To learn more about his creative projects and to sign up for his newsletter see www.jonathanfosteronline.com.

Made in the USA
Middletown, DE
24 September 2021